D1611975

Bury Them Deep in War Smoke

Just after Sam Foster the undertaker has received a letter telling him to have three fresh graves dug, a mysterious man in black arrives in War Smoke with revenge in his heart. Jonas Ward has travelled all the way from the eastern seaboard to fulfil the dying wishes of his late brother Lucas: to kill the three people blamed for Lucas' death. Marshal Matt Fallen enlists the aid of hillbilly Heck Longfellow to try to get to the bottom of the labyrinth of puzzles he is faced with. But can Fallen figure it out in time?

Bury Them Deep in War Smoke

Michael D. George

A Black Horse Western

ROBERT HALE

© Michael D. George 2018
First published in Great Britain 2018

ISBN 978-0-7198-2606-1

The Crowood Press
The Stable Block
Crowood Lane
Ramsbury
Marlborough
Wiltshire SN8 2HR

www.bhwesterns.com

Robert Hale is an imprint
of The Crowood Press

Typeset by
Derek Doyle & Associates, Shaw Heath
Printed and bound in Great Britain by
CPI Group (UK) Ltd, Croydon, CR0 4YY

Dedicated to the lovely Jess George

PROLOGUE

The howling of the locomotive whistle echoed across the massive cattle town of Dodge City as the steam-snorting train readied itself for the long journey to the sprawling settlement of War Smoke. Unlike the vast majority of freight traffic to and from Dodge, this train carried mostly human cargo. There were no cattle cars attached to its tender for this long trek into the depths of the Wild West: a passenger carriage and a baggage car for freight were its only burden.

As darkness fell upon Dodge, a handful of passengers headed towards the railhead to make the long journey. Some had been on casual visits to kinfolk and were returning home, whilst others were cattle agents sent by their wealthy masters to buy the next herd of steers due to arrive in War Smoke within days. On the face of it everything was perfectly normal, but in reality nothing could have been further from the truth.

7

Danger lurked in Dodge City.

Amongst the thousands of people within its boundaries there was a living, breathing creature that barely deserved to be called a man. Most men are not created from pure evil as this one was, yet he, too, was headed for the train depot.

He stood alone in both appearance and motive, about to embark on the long journey to War Smoke. The lean figure was entirely clad in black and built slightly. He wore a gleaming nickel-plated six-shooter in a hand-tooled holster, and his shoulders were draped in a dark trail coat. There was only one reason for him taking the long train ride to War Smoke, and it had nothing to do with buying long-horns or any other more joyous reason: vengeance was bringing the stranger in black to War Smoke – nothing more or less than the desire to kill.

The streets of Dodge City were slowly coming to life, as were the folks who plied their various trades and professions during the hours of night. Darkness was slowly being challenged by the numerous street lanterns that were casting their amber glow through the busy cattle-town's streets. Store windows defied the night as they also sent their coal oil light cascading out on to the sandy streets. Some towns refuse to acknowledge darkness as anything more than nature trying to control humankind and prevent them from enjoying their mutual sins. Dodge City was such a town. Like so many others it wallowed in the fact that it never slept.

8

Yet none of these emotions meant anything to the lean horseman as he steered his tall chestnut stallion silently along the busy thoroughfares towards the rail depot in answer to the beckoning call of the locomotive's whistle. Few cast a second look at the rider as he encouraged his trusty mount ever onward towards its goal. Long shadows stretched out between the array of wooden and brick structures which flanked the gleaming steel tracks.

Since his arrival in Dodge the mysterious man in black had done nothing to draw attention to himself, but now he was getting ready to depart. Now it was time to add another notch to his tally of mutilated victims: it was time to kill again, just to keep in practice. One more kill to tide him over until his true targets were within reach – and that would be his last atrocity until he reached War Smoke.

The horseman in black had only one thought on his mind, and that was to administer his own brand of justice: to avenge what he considered a wrong. Nothing could sway him from what was festering inside his deranged mind. Revenge had grown like a cancer inside him until he no longer had any options available to him but to obey his inner demons.

He had spent his entire life robbing the rich back in the more lucrative sections of New York by using his uncanny ability to scale even the highest building with acrobatic ease. Now he was set on a very different course. Since venturing into the wilds of the West, he had learned that it also paid to be a good shot as well as an acrobatic thief. He had learned quickly that to avenge his brother's execution he would have to become what his late sibling had also become after leaving the eastern seaboard years before: a brutal killer. So far on his long journey he had managed to kill three innocent people and wound double that number. For the man in black it was simply practice – and practice, it is said, makes perfect.

He rode through a narrow alleyway and then turned into a vast open area that stretched out before him. He eased back on his loose leathers and stopped the sturdy stallion beneath him, holding the feisty animal in check as the nagging pain in his skull returned with fearsome wrath. Since he had learned of his brother's fate the pain that had dogged him for most of his life had grown worse. Only the brief exhilaration he had felt with each of his mindless killings seemed to ease the pounding inside his skull momentarily. It was as though the act of killing somehow eased his agony for a few precious heart-beats. But it always returned with a vengeance.

The chestnut stallion stood on the ramp that led down towards the vast ocean of empty cattle pens and the passenger train. His narrowed eyes stared down at the train as he pulled the long stiletto from his boot neck and tested its sharpness with his thumb. No normal man would have considered taking a life so close to the locomotive's scheduled departure, but that was all that filled his mind. He

10

pressed the palm of his hand against his throbbing temple, reached back to his saddle-bag satchel and pulled out a full bottle of wine.

He drove the long thin blade of his deadly knife into the bottle neck and expertly removed its cork in one slick movement. The cold glass neck of the bottle felt good against his dry lips as he downed the entire contents in one long drink. He threw the empty vessel aside, and then heard something to his left.

The horseman in black swung around on his saddle in search of the origin of the noise. He did not have to look for long before he spotted a girl emerge from a shadowy building. Red lantern light spilled out from the half-closed door on to the sand where she stood. He neither knew nor cared who or what she was: all he could think about was killing. A cruel smile etched his features.

Faster than most, he dismounted and led his mount towards the girl; she had halted when she spotted the man, who blended into the dark sur-roundings. But she knew he was moving towards her, and so there was a chance that the night might not be a financial failure after all. She rested her back against the wall of the house and adopted her most alluring pose.

'And who might you be?' she asked, in a well prac-ticed voice that would have worked on anyone else but the man who towered over her. 'You looking for a good time?'

His wry smile grew wider.

'I am,' he rasped, as he loomed over her tiny form. 'That's exactly what I'm looking for – a good time.'

She fluttered her eyelashes at him, and allowed her shawl to drop just a few inches to allow the light that spilled out from the doorway to caress her shoulder.

'The night's early and I got me plenty of time,' she said, as he stopped and inhaled her perfume. 'I got a room inside there. You could spend the night.'

The man in black looked down at her from beneath the brim of his Stetson and sighed heavily. He tilted his head and shook it in answer.

'I ain't got the time, Missy,' he said in a low whisper as he touched her cheek and looked into her eyes. 'I've gotta catch the train down there in the yard. I'm in a hurry to get someplace.'

She looked around his trail coat at the handsome stallion held in his firm grip. Then she made a pitiful stab at looking sad.

'Why'd you wanna take a train when you got yourself such a big, pretty horse, stranger?' she toyed with his bandanna and looked longingly up into his emotionless face. 'Trains are for folks who are just too damn lazy to ride. Let the train go and ride that horse to wherever it is you're headed in the morning. I'm sure better company than the folks on that train will be.'

The man in black leaned down until his face was close to her long dark hair and small ear. He blew at her skin, and she winced as the tickling sensation sent shivers through her.

'I already bought the tickets for me and my tall pretty horse, Missy,' he informed her as he moved closer. 'I'm still going to have myself some fun, though.'

She could tell that she would have to be less subtle if she was going to capture this potential client.

'How can you have any fun without me?' Her hands went south and attempted to make him change his mind. Her smile grew wider as she looked up longingly into his face. Yet no matter how hard she tried, she could not seem to make any difference to the tall man who pinned her seductively to the wall.

'I have my own notion of fun,' he said drily.

'That ain't possible, handsome,' she squeezed him just below his belt buckle and waited for a reaction. 'Together we can make one hell of a lot of fun. All you gotta do is forget about taking that train.'

He glanced down at her busy hands as they continued trying to change his mind. He had never known such flexible fingers, but they were wasting their time, he thought. Then the mind-numbing pain returned to his head and he blinked hard in a vain bid to diminish its tortuous onslaught into his brain.

'I can't do that,' he whispered painfully as he pressed into her. 'I'm headed to War Smoke. I have something mighty important to do there.'

She giggled and looked up innocently into his shadowy face. 'What you gotta do that's so all-fired important in War Smoke? What's more darned important than you and me having us a barrel of fun?'

The man in black looked down into her smiling face.

'I've got to kill the three people who made sure my brother would hang, darling,' he whispered into her neck. 'I gotta make them pay.'

'You're joshing with me,' the girl grinned. 'What's the real reason you're headed to War Smoke? Have you gotta gal there or something?'

He looked at her with a confused expression etched on his face as he fought the incessant pain inside his temple.

'I have to kill three bastards,' he repeated.

Before she could react to his blunt statement he kissed her neck tenderly. Her eyes rolled up under their lids and then closed. She went to kiss him back but a slight jolt forced her back against the wall of the wooden house. At first she imagined that he had just pushed her.

'Steady on there, handsome,' the words had barely left her painted lips when a sudden pain tore through her entire body from just under her left breast. 'What the hell?'

'Ain't that fun?' he smiled.

She blinked rapidly as he backed away from her. The pain grew more intense as she attempted to breathe. Every time she tried to fill her lungs with air she felt as though a boulder had been placed on her chest.

'What's happening?' Then she saw the long-bladed stiletto in his hand. Blood dripped from its honed edge and fell between their feet. Her eyes flashed up at him in disbelief. She tried to speak again, but the only thing that escaped from her mouth was blood. She was drowning in her own blood.

The man in black placed one hand across her mouth to muffle any screams that might alert others of what he had just done. Blood trickled between his fingers for a short time, and then she fell silent. He pulled his hand free and wiped it clean on her shawl.

He had felt her life escaping between his fingers along with her blood, and was exhilarated. The pain inside his temple ebbed and then disappeared as she slid to the ground and crumpled into a sorrowful heap.

He returned his knife to its hiding place, then turned away from his latest victim, gathered up his reins and mounted. With utter disregard for what he had just done, he turned the tall chestnut stallion away and tapped his spurs against its flanks. It covered the distance between the buildings and the brightly lit train quickly, and the horseman had never felt so much power as he did during that short ride.

He raced down through the shadows to the await-ing locomotive as though nothing had just occurred, and was greeted by the train's crew. His narrowed eyes noted that the baggage car door was open and awaiting his trusty horse, a wide wooden ramp having been laid down from the car door to the ground. He eased back on the reins and stopped his mount beside the locomotive crew, his eyes darting between each of the men in turn as though weighing up which of them would be the easiest to kill.

'Hi gentlemen!' he said in his best eastern accent.

The men stared at the eerily strange horseman, unsure as to whether they should be afraid of him or not.

'Are you the critter that booked passage for himself and his horse, mister?' the guard asked, as he tested the ramp with his own weight.

'That'll be me, friend,' the horseman answered.

'You're only just in time,' the porter announced as he watched the horseman dismount. 'We nearly left without you and your horse. Lucky for you I had to go check my timepiece with the depot wall clock, otherwise we'd be long gone by now.'

The narrowed eyes of the ruthless killer watched as his chestnut stallion was led up the ramp into the safety of the baggage car. He pulled out a solid silver cigar case from his pocket and picked out one of its fine Havanas. He bit off its tip and placed it between his teeth and nodded.

'I had business to sort out up in town,' he explained as he returned the case to his pocket, then pulled out a box of matches.

16

'We got a schedule to keep, mister,' the porter grumbled as he paced around the tall stranger and eyed him up carefully. 'We have to keep to time. Otherwise the whole system falls to bits.'

The man looked out from beneath his hat brim at the porter and nodded as the guard came down the ramp. He lifted it and slid it back inside the baggage car, and patted his hands together.

'How'd your business go, stranger?' he asked. The man in black struck a match and lit his cigar.

'I made a killing,' he answered through a cloud of smoke.

CHAPTER ONE

Late the following afternoon the scarlet rays of the sun danced off the numerous window panes along Front Street and created the most dazzling of effects that War Smoke had ever witnessed. For a brief few moments as the sun set across the range it looked as though the remote settlement was ablaze. Then the natural light show ceased, leaving the town bathed in twilight as night slowly approached.

The funeral parlour displayed its finery in large double windows set to either side of a well appointed door. Sam Foster was its proud proprietor, but had been finding the physical side of his job becoming ever harder as he grew older than most of his clients. Because these tasks were now beyond his ageing frame he had hired a couple of far younger and sturdier men to dig the graves and move his lifeless clients around. He was a tall, thin, bald man who had started to look as though he should have been in a coffin rather than hammering nails into them. Yet as with most men in his profession, Sam refused to retire. It was as though he believed that as long as he was burying folks, he was safe from being visited by the Grim Reaper himself.

Sam thought he had experienced most things during his seventy-two years of living, but he had been wrong. A confused frown etched his thin bony face as he sat on a hardback chair outside his parlour.

Heck Longfellow was the total opposite of the always elegantly attired Foster, yet both men had become friends over the years. Longfellow always wore clothes that seemed a few sizes too big for his diminutive body, yet with the aid of a stout rope belt and a cheeky grin, his pants had always remained up. As he strolled across the wide street towards the funeral parlour he noticed that Sam was engrossed with a letter in his hands. Heck knew that the letter must be important because his educated pal was wearing his spectacles. Even as old and bald as the undertaker was, he still retained the vanity of his youth.

'What you reading there, Samuel?' Heck asked as he stepped up under the porch overhang and felt the welcome relief of the shadows. 'Must be plumb interesting the way you keep looking at them words.'

Sam looked up at his friend and nodded in partial agreement with the statement.

'It ain't so much interesting as it is baffling, Heck,' he said with a shake of his head.

Heck had never read anything in his entire life.

He rubbed his neck, leaned over and stared down at the letter. To him it was just like staring at ink scratches on the paper. A pained expression wrinkled up his weathered face as he rested his rear end on the sill of the window behind the hardback chair.

'I thought you could read, Sam,' Heck queried. 'You should be able to figure out them marks.'

Sam turned on his chair and looked up at the puzzled expression on his pal's face. 'Sure I can read it, you old fool. I'm just confused by it.'

Heck grew no wiser.

'Shall I go walk back across to the café and then come on back here so we can start again?' he said in a high-pitched tone that few others could equal in War Smoke. 'If'n you can read them words, you know what it says. That stands to reason, don't it?'

The undertaker stood up beside his scruffy pal and placed a hand on his shoulder.

'I had this letter about a week ago,' he started to explain. 'It tells me to dig three graves up in Boot Hill. It had a fifty-dollar bill pinned to the letter to pay for the work.'

Heck screwed up his eyes.

'I still can't figure out why you're so baffled, Samuel,' he stated with a wave of his hand. 'It sounds pretty damn clear to me. Some *hombre* wanted three graves dug and paid you to have them dug.'

Sam shook the sheet of paper under Heck's nose.

'That's what's bothering me, Heck,' he snapped.

Heck's black bushy eyebrows rose up to his battered hat as he stared at the undertaker in utter confusion. He leaned forwards and looked up into the bald man's face.

'How can that bother you, Samuel?' he asked. 'Some dumb critter paid you to dig three graves. Even I can figure that out, and I can't even read them fancy words.'

Sam edged closer. 'But why would anyone want three graves dug in Boot Hill, Heck? Three fresh dug holes and we ain't got any bodies to plant in them.'

Heck's expression suddenly altered as he thought about the statement. He mumbled to himself and then his jaw dropped.

'Well, whoever that critter is that penned the letter couldn't have mailed the bodies as well, could he?' he groaned as his mind vainly tried to solve the puzzle that had been troubling his friend. 'He'd have needed a damn bigger envelope.'

Totally frustrated, Sam marched into the funeral parlour with his friend tagging behind him. He rested his hands on the marble counter and stared at the letter placed between them, and then vigorously rubbed the paper flat. Yet no amount of flattening of it made it any clearer to comprehend.

'I sent the boys up to the graveyard yesterday and they dug three deep graves just like the letter states,' he told the baggy-panted Heck. 'I took my buggy up there and checked the work a couple of hours back. The boys did a mighty neat job. Just as the letter specifies.'

21

Heck rested his elbows on the marble and looked from under his droopy hat brim at the still perplexed undertaker. He tilted his head and jabbed the paper with his grubby index finger.

'What's the name of the varmint that sent you these instructions, Samuel?' he asked. 'If'n you know his name, I'll go ambulate to wherever he is and ask him why he ordered three graves dug.'

Sam fished the envelope out of his pocket and looked at it carefully. He then raised his eyes and looked at his friend.

'There ain't a return address, Heck,' he stated as he looked closer at the signature at the foot of the written instructions. 'And I can't read the name either.'

Heck adjusted his loose gunbelt and pushed his tongue into his whiskered cheek and shrugged. 'Well, if that don't beat all, Samuel. That critter must be awful trusting, or maybe he's just plain dumb. He sends you fifty dollars and trusts you to do what he wants. For all he knows you might be a sly old critter who'd just spend that fifty dollars and not have any holes dug.'

Sam look horrified. 'I would never do anything so underhanded, Heck.'

'I know that, Samuel,' Heck nodded.

'I paid the boys for the work,' Sam uttered. 'I'm the most honest undertaker in War Smoke. Ask anyone.'

'You're the only undertaker in War Smoke since

old Vernon fell into a grave during a funeral and bust his neck last year, Samuel,' Heck reminded his pal. Suddenly a notion came to Heck. He grinned and pointed at the undertaker.

'That means he knows you, Samuel,' he reasoned. 'Whoever wrote that there letter must know of you. He must know that you're as honest as they come. He figured he could trust you with his fifty bucks.'

Sam straightened up and stared at the dishevelled man leaning on the marble counter, and nodded a few times in agreement. He then looked troubled again, and sighed.

'But who is he?'

Heck jolted upright and placed his fingertips against his mouth as his eyes darted in all directions. He then leaned closer to the thin bald man.

'The question is, why does he want three fresh dug graves up there on Boot Hill, Samuel?' he gulped nervously. 'Who in tarnation does he figure on planting in them holes?'

CHAPTER TWO

Two hours had passed as Heck, the jack-of-all-trades, went about his various jobs around War Smoke. He had cleaned the horse stalls in the livery, helped skin and chop up a variety of animals for the butcher, and had then emptied the spittoons in the Longhorn saloon before scattering a fresh layer of sawdust over its wooden floor. Only as the sun finally began to set did the muttering Heck Longfellow remember that he ought to inform his friend, the marshal, about the strange dilemma that was troubling old Sam in the funeral parlour.

After hitching up his pants and tightening his knotted rope belt, he moved down Front Street at his usual pace. He touched his hat brim to every single person he encountered, adding a few winks for good measure when he passed a female of any age, size or condition. Regardless of his own appearance, Heck drew more than his share of cordial smiles in return. He stomped on the boardwalk outside Marshal Matt

Fallen's office as though attempting to awaken a sleepy leg and then grabbed the door handle and entered.

Fallen greeted his friend with a nod.

Heck dried his nose on his shirt sleeve and grinned broadly at the seated figure of Marshal Matt Fallen as the lawman studied the full cup of coffee before him. The lawman used a pencil to stir the brew as Heck drew closer to him. Heck watched curiously as the marshal kept stirring the black contents of his cup, and his eyes wrinkled up as he wondered why the normally fearless lawman seemed hesitant to drink any of the cup's contents.

'What you doing there, Matthew?' he asked eventually.

Fallen sighed heavily and pointed at the cup.

'What's wrong with this coffee, Heck?' Fallen asked his friend. 'Look at it and tell me what you think.'

Heck sniffed the unusual aroma, gave a suspicious frown and then raised an eyebrow.

'If that was an outhouse I'd reckon it surely needs some lime, Matt,' he whispered. 'Are you sure it's coffee?'

'I'm reasonably sure that's what it's meant to be,' Fallen shrugged doubtfully.

'It don't smell like any coffee I've ever had, Matt,' Heck said before looking around the office the tensely. 'Did Elmer make it?'

Matt sighed, 'Yep.'

'You gonna drink it?'

A pained expression came to the lawman. 'I ain't sure, Heck. That boy keeps experimenting with all sorts of things to put in my coffee. Trouble is, I hate upsetting him. He means well.'

Heck scratched his whiskered chin. 'That boy learned all his cooking skills from his Ma, Matt. That woman is the worst darn cook I ever done met. Starving hound dogs won't eat the scraps she puts out.'

Fallen grinned and pushed the cup into the middle of his ink blotter. 'Coffee ain't meant to have a shine on its surface, is it?'

'Where is Elmer anyways, Matt?' Heck rested a hip on the edge of the desk and stared at the lawman as Fallen kept stirring the black beverage with a pencil. 'He's usually closer than your darn shadow.'

'I sent him home to find his gun,' Fallen sighed. 'That boy never remembers to wear the damn thing. It's peaceful at the moment, but if trouble raises its ugly head, we need our guns. I've bin nagging him to always wear his six-shooter until I'm blue in the face, but he still turns up without it.'

Heck looked knowingly at the lawman.

'I hear that his Ma don't like him wearing a six-shooter, Matthew,' Heck said, tapping the side of his nose. 'I reckon she hides it.'

Matt sighed and then leaned back, and looked at the grizzled man perched on the edge of his desk. He placed his hands behind his head, and stared

26

hard and long at him.

'What brings you to my office, Heck?' he grinned in a bid to change the subject.

'I'm just visiting, Matt,' Heck answered. 'Can't a critter pay a visitation to his best friend?'

Fallen smiled wider.

'Everyone is your best friend, Heck!' he noted.

'Not everybody,' Heck argued. 'It so happens that there are some folks that I hardly think of as my friends, let alone my best friends, Matt.'

The marshal nodded and then noticed the wall clock. Time was marching on and he had things to do. He stared at Heck.

'What exactly do you want, you old galoot?' Fallen asked. 'I've got to go out on my rounds soon. What the hell do you want?'

Heck crossed his legs and looked seriously down at the seated marshal. He sighed, and then scratched his whiskers again as he gathered his thoughts together.

'Why'd I come here?' he wondered aloud. 'Oh yeah, I recall the reason. Old Sam has a real problem that's driving him plumb loco.'

Matt Fallen sat forward. 'Sam the undertaker? What's eating him?'

Heck slowly nodded. 'He's all mixed up down there in his fancy parlour. It seems that some critter wrote him a letter asking him to have three graves dug, up on Boot Hill. Paid him fifty bucks to do it.'

The marshal frowned thoughtfully.

'Who wrote him, Heck?' he enquired.

Heck raised his hands and gave a fruitless gesture.

'I don't know, Matthew,' he sighed. 'Sam don't know either.'

'Has Sam dug the graves?' Fallen stood up, moved round his desk and plucked his Stetson off the hat stand. He flattened his dark hair and then put the hat on as he moved to the door and stared up at the darkening sky.

Heck adjusted his oversized boots, then dropped down from the edge of the desk and trailed the tall lawman to the wide open door.

'Sam got two of his boys to dig the holes yesterday, Matt,' he said as he chewed his bottom lip. 'The thing is, he's plumb scared. He's troubled that he's dug three graves and there ain't anybody to put in the damn things.'

The tall lawman looked down from under the brim of his hat at the far shorter man. He patted Heck on the shoulder.

'I'm obliged that you come and told me about that, Heck,' he said as he continued to study Front Street. 'That is kinda unnerving for the old coot, but there ain't nothing I can do about it.'

Heck winked at Fallen. 'There surely is something you can do, Matthew. You being a law officer, you can investigate.'

'Investigate what exactly?' Fallen sighed as he tucked his thumbs into his belt.

'The grave holes,' Heck suggested with a smile.

28

Fallen raised an eyebrow as he looked down at his friend.

'You want me to go take a look at three holes up on Boot Hill, Heck? Are you serious?' he asked.

'You don't have to go up there yourself, Matt boy,' Heck gave a toothy smile. 'I could go up there and see if anyone shows up.'

The marshal was prepared to agree to anything to get rid of the man with more jobs than anyone else in War Smoke. He rubbed his jaw.

'You just might have something there, Heck,' Fallen said.

'So do you want me to head on up to Boot Hill and keep a lookout around them graves for you, Matt?' Heck asked. 'The varmint that ordered them holes dug might show up. I bet it's someone we know. What do you reckon?'

'You might be right, Heck,' Matt Fallen nodded in acquiescence to his persistent friend. 'Somebody up to no good might have had them graves dug, and he could decide to go and check that Sam has followed his instructions. That could be mighty useful. Yep, you can act as my eyes and ears up at the graveyard.'

Heck Longfellow suddenly beamed with pride and excitement, and clapped his hands together like a child.

'You want me to be like a special deputy?' Heck patted his gun as the holster slid along the well-worn belt until it was hanging like a Scotsman's sporran between his legs. 'A real rootin' tootin' special deputy?'

29

Fallen knew that there was nothing that the scruffy man desired more than being a deputy. He chuckled and then cleared his throat. He nodded firmly.

'Go grab a tin star out of my desk drawer and pin it on, you old galoot,' he drawled. 'I'll pay you fifty cents to keep a lookout for trouble tonight. I reckon there ain't anyone around here that knows them woods around Boot Hill better than you do.'

Heck clapped his hands together. He knew exactly where the lawman kept his tin stars, and had one pinned to his baggy vest within seconds. He strode back to the marshal and gave a nod of his head, and then saluted with his left hand.

'You won't regret this, Matthew,' he declared, as he polished the star with his bandanna tails. 'I ain't lost none of my cunning. I'm still the best there is when it comes to looking out for bad folks.'

'I know there ain't no better, Heck,' Fallen said.

'Whoever that horn-toad is, I'll ferret him out,' Heck said with narrowed eyes.

Fallen closed the office door. The towering frame of the lawman stood on the boardwalk, and watched as Heck scurried toward his saddled mule outside the Longhorn saloon. Fallen shook his head and then locked his office.

'It'll be dark soon,' he muttered, dropping the key into his vest pocket. 'I'd best go get me a cup of real coffee in the café and wait for Elmer so we can do our rounds.'

As he turned back and stepped down on to the

sandy street he observed his newly appointed deputy riding his mule towards Boot Hill. With every stride of his long legs, the marshal thought about what Heck had told him. The more he considered the few facts he knew, the more intrigued he became. Why would anyone want three fresh graves dug? Who was the mysterious writer of the letter? Did he live in War Smoke, or was he somewhere else?

Fallen was filled with questions – questions to which he had no answers. And the more he thought about it, the less clear it became. They say that curiosity killed the cat, but there were times when it was impossible to ignore curious things, and this was one of those times.

He was about to place his pointed boot on the boardwalk outside the café when he paused and glanced over his muscular shoulder at the funeral parlour on the opposite corner of Front Street. It was indeed a strange story, and one that intrigued the tall lawman – and there were few things that Fallen hated more than unsolved puzzles. He knew it would keep gnawing at his craw until he got to the bottom of it. He scratched his chin, and then swung round and proceeded towards the bald old man seated outside the highly elaborate windows, still reading the puzzling letter.

Elmer suddenly appeared and sprinted to the side of the lawman.

'Where we going, Marshal Fallen?' he asked.

'I'm going to have me a chinwag with old Sam,' he

said firmly; then looking down at his still unarmed deputy, said 'And you're going to the office to get a scattergun.'

'Why do I need me a scattergun for?' Elmer asked fearfully. Fallen narrowed his eyes.

'Because you forgot your six-gun again,' he said firmly, 'That's why.' Elmer was about to say something else when he felt the marshal's large hand clip him behind his ear. He halted his progress and whined 'What you do that for, Marshal Fallen?' as he vigorously rubbed the back of his head. Fallen grinned at his hapless deputy.

'I'll tell you later, Elmer,' he said, as he continued on towards the funeral parlour. 'I ain't had time to think of a reason yet.'

CHAPTER THREE

The sprawling township of War Smoke was eerily quiet as it turned midnight. The countless saloons and gambling houses were still busy, as were the various dwellings of ill repute that were scattered around the moonlit settlement. Trade was ticking along at its usual pace as Marshal Matt Fallen and his deputy Elmer Hook turned into Front Street and walked back to their office set halfway along the wide thoroughfare.

As the six-and-a-half-foot tall marshal strode purposely through the lantern light and shadows, Elmer shuffled nervously beside him, toting a scattergun across his lean belly. Fallen was tired and looking forward to a few hours shuteye on a cot inside one of his empty jail cells, while Elmer thought about a tall glass or two of suds, drooling in anticipation.

'It sure is darn peaceful tonight, Marshal Fallen,' he noted as they crossed a side street and then continued their walk. 'Makes a man thirsty.'

Fallen glanced down at his much shorter companion and smiled as he adjusted his hat. 'What does, Elmer?'

Elmer looked and grinned at his mentor.

'I said walking makes a man thirsty,' he repeated.

Fallen stopped and rested the palm of his hand on his holstered gun grip, and sighed as he rubbed his powerful jaw thoughtfully. He still could not get his mind off the letter that Sam Foster had shown him hours earlier. He glanced beyond the array of brightly lit saloons and gambling halls at Boot Hill, and silently thought about Heck.

'What you thinking about, Marshal Fallen?' Elmer asked as he held on to the massive double-barrelled shotgun.

'I was just thinking about Heck,' the lawman replied.

Elmer raised his eyebrows.

'Why would you be thinking about that old egg sucker for?'

Fallen hid his amusement and turned away from his scrawny young deputy. 'That's no way to be talking about a fellow deputy, Elmer.'

Elmer's expression changed. 'Since when has Heck bin a deputy, Marshal Fallen?'

'Since just before sundown.' The lawman answered. 'Heck was there when I needed a job done, and he jumped at the chance to help me out.'

'You made him a deputy?' Elmer croaked.

Fallen nodded firmly. 'You were off looking for

your gun, as I recall.'

Elmer had always prided himself on being a deputy marshal, and did not like the notion that he had competition. He rubbed his throat and sidled up to the thoughtful Fallen.

'I'm awful thirsty, Marshal Fallen,' he repeated. 'I'm even thirstier than I was before I learned that Heck has been made a deputy.'

'Special deputy, Elmer,' Fallen corrected, as his fingers fumbled in his pocket. The high-shouldered marshal pulled his pocket watch from his vest pocket and flicked its lid open. He moved under a street light, and its amber light lit up the face of the time-piece. The marshal nodded and then snapped the lid shut before returning it to his pocket.

'It's only just turned midnight,' Fallen nodded. 'I reckon it's still early.'

Elmer gripped his shotgun excitedly. 'You mean we can go and have us a few drinks, Marshal Fallen?'

Fallen stretched his massive arms and then grinned.

'Sure,' he sighed. 'Reckon old Doc Weaver might still be in the Longhorn about now.'

Elmer's face lit up. 'I'm sure glad you thought about us having a few drinks, Marshal. My finances are a bit stretched at this time o' the month.'

The two figures stepped down from the boardwalk and began the slow walk towards the Longhorn Saloon. Lantern light and piano music washed out through its swing doors in greeting as the lawmen approached their favoured drinking hole.

'Are you broke again, Elmer?' Fallen asked, as his keen senses continued to study the quiet street. 'You were paid last Friday, like me. How can you get through your wages even before you get them?'

They weaved through a dozen saddle horses tied to a hitching pole, ducked under its twisted length and then stepped up on to the boardwalk. Fallen rested a hand on the top of the swing doors and paused as he waited for a reply from his young friend, who was still drooling at the thought of having a few drinks. Elmer dried his mouth on his sleeve and looked up into the marshal's face.

'I got me a whole heap of overheads, Marshal Fallen,' he stated, waving his long double-barrelled weapon around. 'You can't imagine how plumb expensive it is nowadays for a *hombre* on deputy wages. It ain't like it was in your time.'

Fallen narrowed his eyes.

'How old do you reckon I am, Elmer?' he drawled.

The deputy raised his eyebrows and studied his superior carefully, before shrugging and looking at his boot leather coyly. 'You gotta be pretty old.'

Fallen removed his hat and ran his fingers through his mop of thick black hair before returning the Stetson. 'Old? I'm only just a tad over thirty. I bet you're almost as old as me!'

'I surely doubt that, Marshal Fallen,' Elmer blurted. Matt Fallen began to nod, and Elmer forced a sheepish grin.

'I'm still awful thirsty, Marshal,' he reminded his superior. 'War Smoke is getting so damn big that it's plumb tuckering, walking our rounds nowadays.'

'It was much smaller in my day,' the lawman joshed. 'When I got here it was just a tent, two hound dogs and a spittoon.'

The lawmen entered the saloon and wandered through the cloud of tobacco smoke. They navigated a route between card tables and bargirls to the long bar counter where Doc Weaver was hunched over an empty glass. It was obvious the elderly doctor was low on funds and weighing up if he should buy another drink or not. His wrinkled eyes caught the reflections of the lawmen in the mirror set behind the bartender.

'It's about time you got here, Matt,' Doc grumbled as he toyed with his empty whiskey glass. 'A man could die of dehydration waiting for you.'

'I'm sorry, Doc,' Fallen patted the old-timer on his back and pointed to the bartender. 'Elmer drags his feet a lot lately. The boy gets slower every day.'

The bartender caught Fallen's attention.

'Two beers, Marshal?' Slim Cooper asked the towering lawman.

'And a whiskey for Doc, Slim,' Fallen nodded as he rested a boot on the brass rail that fronted the wooden counter between spittoons.

'Thank you kindly, Matt,' Doc said as he turned his wrinkled face to greet the marshal. 'It's damn quiet in town tonight.'

37

'It sure is, Doc,' Fallen agreed. 'Too damn quiet for my liking. I don't like it when it's this peaceful.'

'Trouble's brewing someplace,' Doc said as he watched the bartender fill his glass with amber liquor. 'I can feel it my bones.'

Fallen tossed a silver dollar into the bartender's hands and pushed one of the glasses to Elmer, who gratefully raised it to his mouth and started guzzling.

'I'd have figured that you'd relish trouble, Doc,' Matt said after taking a swallow of beer. 'The more trouble, the more money you make.'

Doc raised his bushy eyebrows as he sipped his whiskey and nodded. 'That's true, Matt. Trouble is, I'm getting old. I get plumb tuckered when things get too cantankerous around here.'

Fallen fished two dollars out of his pocket and dropped them into his old friend's jacket breast pocket.

'What's that for?' Doc asked stroking his white moustache with his fingers.

'Don't you recall that gunslinger who called me out last week, Doc?' Fallen downed the rest of his beer and pushed his glass towards the bartender. 'I forgot to pay you your fee for confirming the critter was dead.'

Doc eyed his tall pal: 'Much obliged.'

'Two more beers, Slim!' the marshal indicated to Cooper.

Doc patted his pocket and heard the coins rattling against one another. 'I forgot all about that idiot.

That boy was fast, but not fast enough.'

'Apart from that idiot, War Smoke has bin damn quiet for months, Doc,' Fallen tossed another dollar at Slim as two more beers were placed before them. 'I don't like it when it's too quiet. Makes me edgy.'

'A little bird tells me that you were talking to old Sam earlier, Matt,' Doc sighed. 'How come?'

'Just something Heck told me about,' Fallen said, his large hand rubbing the nape of his neck. 'Sam got himself a letter with fifty dollars in it. He was instructed to have three graves dug up on Boot Hill.'

'Fifty dollars?' Doc gasped enviously. 'The lucky bastard. I can't recall the last time I had that much money. I knew I should have been an undertaker instead of a quack.'

Elmer leaned around Fallen, 'What you both talking about?'

'Suck on them suds, boy,' Doc chuckled.

Fallen studied the busy saloon. It was still busy, and yet unusually quiet. He shook his head thoughtfully.

'Folks are real peaceable again,' he sighed.

Doc drained his glass and turned to face the room full of patrons. A wry smile came to the veteran medical man as he adjusted his jacket and pulled his black derby down towards his spectacles.

'I'll be wishing you a fond goodnight, boys,' he grinned as he started towards the swing doors. 'I'm off to my cot.'

Elmer nudged Fallen like an annoying mosquito until he finally got the lawman's attention. The tall marshal glanced down on the smiling deputy.

'What do you want now, Elmer?' he drawled. It then became obvious that Elmer was staring at one of the bargirls. Fallen shook his head and rested a paw on his deputy. 'Has she got teeth? Most of the gals in here ain't got teeth.'

Elmer looked offended.

'They all got teeth, Marshal Fallen!' he said with a nod of his head.

'I'll take your word for that,' Fallen shrugged. 'You seem to know most of them better than most.'

'Can I have me a sub on my wages, Marshal Fallen?' Elmer whispered as he took another swig from his beer.

'How much?' Fallen sighed.

'Three dollars oughta be enough,' Elmer calculated, as suds dripped off his chin. 'I'm gonna sweet-talk Miss Diana.'

Fallen glanced at the attractive girl, then fished out three silver dollars from his vest and handed them to the deputy. The coins had only just landed in the palm of Elmer's hand when the deputy darted through the crowd after the bargirl.

The marshal looked at Slim and beckoned for another glass of beer. As the fresh brew was placed before the tall lawman the bartender leaned over the damp counter towards Fallen.

'That boy has got more sap than a maple tree, Marshal,' Slim laughed as he mopped the counter surface with a rag. 'He's chased every one of the girls in here and caught a few by all accounts.'

'As long as that's all he's caught,' the lawman sighed.

Slim grinned at the lawman. 'I ain't seen you sniffing around any of my girls' petticoats for the longest while, Marshal. You ain't got religion, have you?'

Fallen took a mouthful of beer. 'I'm just biding my time for a while, Slim.'

The bartender served a couple of the cowboys a few feet along the bar and then returned to the lawman, as Fallen watched his deputy trailing the attractive bargirl around the busy establishment.

'I can't figure how Elmer can afford all the gals he chases, Matt,' he wondered as he polished thimble glasses and started to stack them.

'I know exactly how he can afford it, Slim,' Fallen said.

'How?' the bartender pressed.

'With all the subs on his wages, I reckon Elmer earns more money than I do, Slim.' Fallen sighed wistfully.

'Don't you deduct it from his wages?' Slim asked.

'By my figuring he's already borrowed so much that he'll still be owing me two years after he's dead,' Fallen grinned, and glanced at the reflection of his romantic deputy wrapped around the laughing girl.

Fallen finished his beer, straightened up, touched the brim of his hat and then picked up the scattergun, which Elmer had deserted, off the bar counter and started for the street.

41

'See you, Slim,' he said before pushing his way through the swing doors and continuing his journey back towards his office. As he mounted the opposite boardwalk he glanced around the street before entering the lantern-lit office. He was still thinking about his other deputy – the special deputy who was watching the three new graves in hope of discovering who had paid for them to be dug. Heck was a seasoned mountain man, and Fallen had no fear that anything would happen to him. Yet a nagging thought continued to haunt his tired mind: what was going on?

After talking to Sam, the marshal was no wiser. This was indeed a puzzle, and Fallen did not like puzzles. They troubled him and disturbed his sleep. At least War Smoke was quiet, he thought, as he tossed his hat on to the tall stand and closed the door wearily behind him. Fallen moved around his desk and placed the scattergun on the wall rifle rack beside the variety of other rifles. He then turned back to his desk, adjusted the brass wheel of the lamp and dimmed its illumination before adjusting his gunbelt and sprawling out on the cot inside the first jail cell.

Normally Fallen would have unbuckled the gunbelt, but something deep in his fretful mind told him to keep it strapped to his hips. He lay on the cot and stared up at the ceiling as his aching body adjusted to the mattress. He was tired, but still that nagging thought kept troubling him: it was like the calm before the storm.

He was too experienced just to accept the quiet times without trepidation. He knew everything had a price tag, and that included the relatively peaceful periods of time which always came before something bad replaced them. Matt Fallen's unrivalled experience told him that War Smoke was about to erupt like a volcano, and when it did, nothing and nobody was safe in the sprawling town. He could see images in his mind of the freshly dug graves, and brooded about why anyone might be having them dug. He concluded it was a warning that at least three souls would soon meet their Maker.

It was a threat. But who was being threatened?

And more importantly, who was doing the threatening? Sweat trailed down the face of the lawman as he tossed and turned on the far-too-small cot. He was exhausted and needed a few hours' shuteye, but could not seem to stop his over-active mind from posing unanswerable questions.

Trouble was indeed brewing, Marshal Fallen reasoned. It always was, in a town like War Smoke. Like tinder-dry brush, the merest spark could ignite it, and it would be up to him to clean up the mess. All he could do was wait until he was called upon to act. It gnawed at his craw, and even after all the years that he had worn a star on his chest, he was still not used to it. The waiting was always the worst. But the decent folks of War Smoke relied upon him, and that was a heavy burden, even for his wide shoulders to carry.

Matt Fallen closed his eyes and allowed the calming effects of the beer to settle him. Yet even as he fell into the depths of sleep, he was still ready for action, his right hand resting on his holstered gun grip, his fingers curled around it in readiness. He twisted and turned on the far-too-small cot as a hundred troubling notions flashed through his dreams. He hadn't enjoyed a restful slumber for months, and this night would be no different.

CHAPTER FOUR

No snorting bull about to charge at a matador could have appeared more awesome than the tall, black metal monster as it slowly emerged through the night mist on its approach to the train depot at War Smoke. Red-hot sparks of burning cinders rose from its stack into the night and mingled with the cloud of grey smoke that marked its path, billowing upwards in hesitant bursts.

The hissing of steam escaping around the massive locomotive sounded like a rattlesnake nest when its occupants begin their nightly ritual and ready their fangs in anticipation of fresh prey. From a distance the large black locomotive resembled a mythical dragon moving through the outskirts of War Smoke. A beam of light carved down from its high perch and illuminated the steel rails supporting the train's tremendous bulk.

The giant black monster snaked its way through the outskirts of the sprawling settlement towards its goal, every turn of its huge wheels bringing it ever closer to the train depot. As was usual, the train was an hour overdue as it drew nearer to the brightly lit array of wooden structures a few hundred yards from the empty cattle pens. This part of War Smoke was bathed in shadow, apart from the occasional red lanterns that hung outside certain of its more popular properties.

An ear-splitting whistle broke the eerie silence as the train finally groaned to a halt. As steam gushed from around the long black locomotive the engineer leaned out from the footplate and looked back at the solitary passenger car and the windowless guard's van hooked up behind it. To even the most ignorant of eyes it was obvious that this was not a freight train ready to load cattle into its caravan of fragrant cars and transport them back east: this was a passenger train.

Both the driver and his engineer disembarked from their high perch behind the firebox and wandered into one of the wooden buildings set thirty feet away. As they disappeared into the ticket office the train conductor slowly descended the steps and jumped down the last few feet to the dusty ground. He placed a wooden box on the ground to make the last step less bone-jerking for his paying passengers. Roughly thirteen men and women made their way down to the ground and proceeded out into the shadowy surroundings as the conductor checked his time-piece and waited for the last of his human cargo to disembark.

The last man to leave the brightly lit car was unlike the others who had got off before him down the metal steps. He looked far taller than his actual six feet as he stopped beside the conductor and placed a long slim cigar between his lips. Clad entirely in black with a long matching top coat resting over his shoulders, Jonas Ward gave the appearance of being a sophisticated soul.

Nothing could have been further from the truth.

Ward was dangerous. Every pore of his elegant body oozed danger as he struck a match and cupped its flame to his cigar and inhaled.

'My horse is back in there, conductor,' Ward smiled, as smoke filtered back through his gritted teeth. He shook the match and flicked it away casually as the conductor checked his notes and nodded in agreement.

'So it is,' the far shorter man said, pacing to the guard's van and hammering on its locked door. 'Open up, Charlie. I got me a gentleman out here that wants his horse.'

The words had barely left the conductor's lips when the sound of bolts being released filled the air. Ward stepped back and watched as the large door was slid open to reveal the interior of the car. A large man touched his peaked cap and then started to push a board out from the car to use as a ramp.

'Do you have business in War Smoke?' the conductor asked as the guard continued to secure the wide board.

Ward sucked in smoke and nodded.

'You could say that, friend,' he replied drily.

The conductor sensed that it was far wiser not to pursue this line of smalltalk. He looked around the empty cattle yard, and then studied the stranger wearing the flat-brimmed black Stetson.

'You ever bin to War Smoke before?' he ventured.

Ward's eyes darted over to the conductor; he could hear his horse's hoofs as it was led to the hastily constructed ramp.

'Nope, I've never bin here before,' he answered as the flame face of his tall chestnut stallion emerged into the torchlight.

'You'll like War Smoke,' the conductor said, as he tucked his pencil behind his ear. 'It's a wonderful place. Got everything a real man needs. Saloons, gambling halls and plenty of brothels.'

Ward nodded as he exhaled smoke at the ground.

'What about wine?' he asked as the guard carefully led the chestnut down the ramp to the ground and handed its reins to the tall man in black.

The conductor raised his eyebrows. 'Wine?'

'Yeah, wine,' Ward nodded as he handed a silver dollar to the guard and stroked the neck of his nervous horse. 'Has War Smoke got good wine?'

Both the guard and the conductor glanced at one another in mutual confusion. They shrugged at the question as Ward checked his handsome horse.

'Me and Charlie here tend to drink beer,' he said.

'Folks around here are much the same, though I reckon you could find wine in some of the fancier saloons.'

Ward gripped his saddle horn and stepped in his stirrup, and mounted his high-shouldered horse. He gathered up his reins and looked down at both men as they struggled to push the large ramp back into the car, then touched his black brim.

'Much obliged,' he said before turning his mount. 'I reckon it's time I taught this town a few things.'

The conductor smiled up at the mysterious horse-man.

'You'll find it awful hard to teach these folks to appreciate wine, mister,' he said. 'They're set in their ways. Beer and rye is all they know.'

Jonas Ward held his horse in check. He swung around. His face was totally emotionless as he glared at them, and his icy stare matched his voice.

'I'm not talking about wine, friend,' he said, as he pulled back the long tails of his coat to reveal a hol-stered gun with an ivory grip. He stroked the six-shooter: 'There's some folks in War Smoke I've got to teach a few other things to first.'

The two men swallowed hard. Neither spoke.

Ward drove his spurs into the flanks of his stallion and rode off towards the centre of War Smoke. As dust rose up into the lantern-lit darkness, the railway employees looked at one another.

'Who in tarnation is that critter, Jeb?' the guard asked.

The conductor rubbed his neck and loosened his starched collar. 'I don't know, and between you and me, I don't wanna know.'

'He be darn creepy,' the guard muttered as he slid the car door and rested his knuckles on his hips. 'That *hombre* got me shaking.'

'Let's join the other boys and down us some coffee, Charlie,' the conductor suggested. 'My throat feels like it just argued with a straight razor.'

'I need me something far stronger than coffee,' the other railwayman uttered, and pulled a slim hipflask from his pants pocket, unscrewed its stopper and took a swig. As its fiery contents burned a trail down into his innards he handed the flask to the conductor.

'You're right,' the conductor said, raising the metal container to his lips.

CHAPTER FIVE

The moonlit hill that loomed over the settlement had been dubbed Boot Hill, like countless others throughout the West. A hundred or more headstones and wooden markers covered the area set in a clearing beside a wood. The graves of some bodies had been marked with a simple wooden cross consisting of two snapped branches, as folks either did not know the name of the corpse or, more often, no longer cared. The wealthier of the bodies laid to rest had their names chiselled on stone, as though that gave them a guarantee of immortality. Yet when everything is weighed up, death is simply death, the final ride to a place that nobody knows.

War Smoke was still busy below the hillside as Heck Longfellow looked down from his hiding place. By this time he had been nestled there for three hours, and he knew that apart from wild critters that had curiously passed by his hastily constructed lair, he was alone. At least, that was what he thought.

There had not been a single sign that any other man was anywhere close to where he and his mule were secreted. He looked out through wrinkled eyes at the eerily lit hill, which stretched down to the very outskirts of War Smoke, and started to feel his stomach groaning. He was both hungry and thirsty, and he knew that this was the hardest fifty cents he would ever earn.

'Hush up, belly,' he whispered at his growling guts. He got to his feet cautiously, and crouched as his eyes stared out through the leafy brush behind the countless markers. He then turned and moved back to his mule, opened up its saddle-bags and scooped out some horse biscuits. He scattered them on the ground before the animal and watched as it began to consume them happily. 'My, you sure make them look appetizing, Nellie gal.'

Heck began to lick his lips as he watched the mule devouring its rations. As it continued to pluck the biscuits off the ground, Heck rubbed his noisy belly again. 'They sure looks awful nice the way you tuck into them, gal.'

Then the urge to try them overwhelmed him, and he poked his nose into the satchel, sniffed at the loose horse biscuits, and dipped his hand into them. He retrieved a few and popped them into his mouth, and bit down hard – they were surprisingly tough. It was hard to figure out exactly what the flavour of the biscuits was actually meant to be, but whatever it was, it was not to his taste. His expression changed as the taste spread like a wildfire around his mouth. Coughing, he spat the crushed remnants at the ground in disgust, and frantically kept spitting in a vain attempt to rid his mouth of the taste.

'Holy moonshine,' Heck moaned. 'How can you eat them things, Nellie?' He glowered at the mule as he wiped his tongue on the back of his sleeve, while it continued to munch on the remaining biscuits at its hoofs. 'They taste like a hound dog's hind leg,' he muttered, and took a swig from his canteen. Yet even that could not wash the flavour from his tongue. 'Them things are so bad they make Elmer's coffee seem like a delicacy.'

Heck looped the canteen back on to his saddle, then dropped back on to his knees and crawled through the undergrowth to his lookout place. He was about to grumble again when he spotted something moving towards the cemetery through the bright moonlight. He squinted: it took a few moments for his eyes to adjust to it, then back to the eerie light it cast over the countless markers and headstones. Then it dawned on Heck what he was looking at.

The rider did not resemble anyone Heck recognized, and he knew practically everyone in War Smoke. The hairs on the nape of his neck began to tingle as he lowered himself down on to his still grumbling belly and pushed the grass away from his face. He squinted through the parted weeds.

The horseman entered the graveyard, then pulled

53

back on his looped reins to stop his mount's progress. Jonas Ward rose in his stirrups, then swung his long leg over the cantle of his saddle and dismounted in a well practised action. He kept his head low so that the shadows hid his features from anyone who might cast their eyes in his direction. When satisfied that he was alone in the graveyard he led the stallion to the boundary and securely tied its reins to the picket fence that encircled the clearing.

He might have been alone in the graveyard – but every movement was observed by the hidden special deputy in the undergrowth. Ward strode from his mount to the freshly dug graves: his piercing eyes studied the deep holes and the mounds of soil piled up beside them.

Heck strained to see, but it was impossible for him to identify the stranger clad entirely in black, particularly as the flat brim of Ward's hat prevented the moonlight from illuminating his features.

'Who the hickory is that fella?' Heck said in a hushed whisper. 'I don't recognize that critter at all. He sure don't look like anyone I've ever seen before in town.'

Then as if he had heard something, Ward raised his head and looked around the graveyard. Heck pressed his face into the mud and from his hiding place, watched the stranger in black. Ward walked around the three graves like a military man inspecting his troops. Then he moved away from the freshly disturbed ground and strode to the corner of the graveyard, and stopped beside one of the wooden markers.

Heck raised himself up a little and looked over a pile of weeds at the man in the long black trail coat. His mind desperately attempted to recognize him, but Ward had turned his back on the deputy. Heck wondered what he was doing. He had never seen anyone like Jonas Ward before, and the stranger frightened him.

As though in silent prayer, Jonas Ward stared down at the crude inscription on the wooden board. It was written in black paint. Then he began to nod his head up and down as he made a silent vow – a promise that could only be heard by the spirit of the man buried beneath the wooden marker. After a few seemingly endless moments he turned and marched purposefully back to his horse.

It was like watching some demonic creature, Heck thought as he stared at Ward. The long tails of the stranger's black trail coat floated around his lean frame in a similar fashion to the robes of a priest.

Yet this was no priest, Heck reasoned. This was something he had never encountered before. Something far darker.

Ward reached the chestnut stallion and pulled its reins free of the fence. He then reached up to the saddle horn, stepped into the closest stirrup, and in one fluid action was back in the saddle. He dragged the reins hard to his right and spurred the handsome animal down the hillside. The stallion carved a route through the moonlight as it made its way back down towards War Smoke.

Heck Longfellow rose up from his hiding place and pushed his way back out of the bushes. He watched the horseman steer his mount back towards the glowing lights of the settlement, a cloud of wispy dust rising up into the moonlight in its wake. Totally bemused, Heck rubbed the mud off his rugged features and shook his head. He wasn't sure what he had just witnessed. All he knew for sure was that he should tell Matt Fallen as quickly as possible.

'Nellie,' he called out, and ran back into the undergrowth after his trusty mule. He pulled the rope securing the mule to a tree and dragged it out of the shadows. 'We gotta go tell Matt about this. Maybe he'll be able to figure out who that *hombre* is.'

Heck clambered on to the animal and shook the reins feverishly. Taking great care not to be observed by the horseman ahead of him, Heck steered the stubborn mule between the markers and gravestones and out of the cemetery. He pulled back on his reins and watched Ward as he rode towards the outskirts of War Smoke.

Heck pulled the long reins hard to his left and tapped his boot leather against the flanks of the mule. He rode into the long grass and then whipped the animal's tail. The mule responded instantly to the encouragement and started down the steep incline. Heck knew that even if the unknown rider were to look back, he would not have any idea that

56

he was being trailed. The mule trotted onwards, with Heck somehow maintaining his balance on the crude saddle as they quickly descended the steep moonlit hillside.

Heck stretched up and peered over the top of the high waving grass. He caught a brief glimpse of the horseman as Ward steered his stallion into War Smoke. Realizing he was now safe from prying eyes, the one-time gold prospector rode back up on to the less taxing grassy slope.

'Come on, Nellie gal,' Heck urged the mule as he polished his deputy star with his loose cuff. 'We gotta go tell Matthew what we found out.'

CHAPTER SIX

The chestnut stallion had slowed to a walk as it entered Front Street. It meandered along the relatively empty street as Ward studied the scattering of souls still wandering from one den of pleasure to the next. His cold, calculating eyes didn't miss a trick as the handsome horse continued on past the various saloons and gambling halls. Nothing escaped the notice of the mysterious Jonas Ward as he turned up passed the corner café and headed towards the livery stable.

A lone lantern hung just below the hay-loft door and above the tall barn doors. A glowing light flickered its red glory across the interior of the stable as Ward drew rein outside the large building. He dismounted, keeping hold of the long reins as a stout man emerged from the structure and looked at the stranger in black. His eyes went from Ward's boots and did not stop until they reached the black Stetson.

'Howdy, stranger,' the large blacksmith said in a deep drawl. 'I ain't seen you before around these parts.'

Ward smiled the way card sharps smile when they don't want you to know how good a hand they're holding before raising the stakes.

'I just got to town about an hour back,' Ward said as he followed the muscular man into the livery stable. A dozen horses were stalled around the back wall close to the warm forge.

'You and your horse are looking mighty neat considering how far you must have ridden, stranger,' the wily man noted, resting his hefty form on the edge of the forge. He warmed his hands over the red hot coals, then looked back at the menacing man in black. 'That's a real clever trick and no mistake.'

Ward toyed with the reins and inhaled deeply.

'I didn't ride all the way here from the next town,' he admitted before tilting his head and staring at the large man who watched him like a hawk. 'But you've already figured that out. I came in on the train. My horse was in the baggage car.'

'I figured as much, stranger,' Jed Hansen nodded before rising again and moving towards Ward and his horse. He placed a hand on the neck of the tall animal and then stared at it. 'You didn't come straight here from the railyard though, did you?'

Ward raised an eyebrow.

'How can you tell that?' he asked curiously.

The blacksmith stroked the horse's nose. 'I don't

know much but I know horses. This fella has started a sweat. Not a bad one like an animal that's ridden ten or so miles. He has only just started to warm up. You must have taken a ride around War Smoke before you came here. Am I right?'

Ward nodded.

'Dead right,' he acknowledged. 'We did have a little ride around the town to loosen him up. He was standing in that train car for a couple of hours and got stiff. Like most stallions he gets ornery unless you tire him.'

Hansen looked at the horse: 'He's a fine animal. You don't see many like him in these parts. Folks don't tend to look after their animals too good around here. You obviously value this tall critter.'

Ward nodded again.

'That's right,' he agreed. 'I value horseflesh. This horse can outrun most other nags. That's pretty handy in my line of work.'

Jed Hansen stared at the man beside him. Although the elegant figure seemed to pose no threat, like so many of the men who drifted in and out of War Smoke, there was something about Ward which was not as it first appeared. The blacksmith sensed that Ward was dangerous. He took hold of the horse's bridle and then cast his eyes at the lean stranger.

'What is your line of work, stranger?' Hansen grinned.

The crimson light of the forge spilled across the

vast interior of the fragrant livery stable and danced across the figure clad entirely in black. Ward tilted his head back and stared hauntingly at the black-smith.

'I'm a drummer, friend,' he lied, turning on his heels and releasing his saddle-bags from their restraints. 'I sell things to local stores.'

Hansen gave a knowing nod of his head.

'I've met a lot of drummers over the years, and none of the critters looked like you,' he remarked.

Ward slung the bags over his shoulder as a smile etched his face. He fished out a few coins from his coat pocket and handed them to the blacksmith. He then touched the brim of his black Stetson.

'That oughta cover the cost of you looking after my horse for a couple of days,' he mumbled before pushing the tails of his long trail coat over his hol-stered gun grip. The nickel-plated weapon was almost as impressive as the chestnut stallion.

'You only gonna stay in town for two days?' Hansen asked as he expertly unsaddled the animal and placed the saddle over a stall wall.

'I reckon so,' Ward pulled out a silver cigar case and opened its lid as he watched the large man turn the stallion into one of the numerous stables. The man in black took out a cigar and placed it between his teeth, then closed the highly polished case and returned it to his pocket. 'Two days should be enough.'

'Enough for what?' the blacksmith grinned.

'Enough for me to complete my business, friend,' Ward struck a match with his thumbnail and raised the flickering flame to the cigar. He inhaled the strong smoke and then blew the flame out with a line of grey smoke. 'Are there any good hotels in this town?'

The blacksmith nodded as he dropped a pile of hay at the hoofs of the stallion. He marched through the eerie light to the barn doors and pointed towards the middle of War Smoke.

'You'll find a couple of hotels down yonder on Front Street, stranger,' he said as Ward strode to his side with the cigar gripped firmly between his teeth. His cold, calculating stare surveyed the moonlit structures with interest. He pulled the cigar from his mouth and blew a line of smoke into the crisp air.

'Do any of them have a supply of good wine?' he asked the sweating blacksmith, before turning to look at him. Hansen raised his bushy eyebrows.

'You mean that stuff Frenchies drink?' he asked.

Ward nodded. 'The very same, friend. I have a weakness for good wine. I don't care too much for what passes for whiskey or beer in these parts. I like fine wine.'

'I reckon the Diamond Pin Hotel is your best bet to find fancy liquor,' the blacksmith shrugged. 'I'm only guessing though. I ain't ever seen anyone drinking the stuff.'

'Thank you kindly, friend,' Ward touched the brim of his hat again and started to walk back towards the heart of War Smoke. 'I'll go find out for myself.'

Jed Hansen rubbed the sweat off his face with the palm of his large hand, and shook his head a few times. He did not take his eyes off Ward as the man in black moved through the moonlight towards his goal. The blacksmith exhaled loudly and walked back inside the livery stable, pausing for a few moments as he watched the handsome stallion eating the hay. Then he turned and looked back out into the moonlit street as Ward walked out of view around a corner. The burly liveryman sat down next to his warm forge.

Although Hansen thought that he had never met the stranger before, there was something about Ward which troubled him. There was something familiar about him that the blacksmith couldn't quite put his finger on.

'That *hombre* unsettles me, but I'm damned if I can figure out why,' he announced to the horses in their individual stables.

CHAPTER SEVEN

The small man seated behind the large desk in the foyer of the Diamond Pin looked up from his newspaper as the street door opened and Jonas Ward entered the brightly illuminated building; the sound of his rattling spurs echoed around the plush surroundings as he slowly made his way to the desk. The slightly built clerk rose to his full, if unimpressive height, and rested his shaking hands on the large register.

'Welcome to the Diamond Pin, sir,' he stammered, vainly searching for enough spittle to swallow. He took a pen from its stand and dipped it into the inkwell. 'Do you wish to register?'

Ward looked down at the fearful man through his cigar smoke, and then nodded. He took the pen from the twitching hand and swung the large book round. He then scrawled an indecipherable signature on the page, and dropped the pen back on the table.

The clerk moved the book back round to face him. He couldn't make out the name, and loosened his starched collar. No matter how hard he tried, the tiny man could not take his eyes off the stranger. He had never seen anyone that looked anything like Ward before. Clad all in black with smoke billowing from his lips, Ward looked like something he had only ever read about in dime novels.

'Do you have any preference where you might like a room, sir?' the clerk asked fearfully.

'A room facing the street would be best,' Ward replied.

The clerk turned and stared at the rack of wooden pigeon holes, and the key that hung from a hook beside each one. He plucked one off its hook, and placed it down on the register; the number three was painted on a metal tag hanging from it.

'This room is directly above the foyer, sir,' the clerk said, as he pointed a shaking finger upwards. 'It has a perfect view of Front Street.'

Ward took the key, and looked around the well-appointed interior of the hotel. His eyes then darted back to the clerk, and he rested a hand on the desk.

'Tell me, friend,' he drawled ominously. 'Does this hotel have any fine wine in its cellar?'

The small clerk nodded in startled surprise by the question.

'Yes indeed, sir. We've got a lot of wine,' he answered. 'The previous owner bought a lot of the stuff before he was killed.'

Ward reached into his pocket and produced a wad of bank notes and then peeled off a few of them. He handed them to the clerk.

'Bring five bottles of red to my room,' he demanded, before turning and walking to the staircase.

The clerk looked at the notes in his hands, and then looked to Ward's wide back as he slowly made his way to the landing.

'But this is too much,' he called out. 'Way too much.'

Ward reached the top of the stairs and then paused. He turned his head and looked over the saddle-bags on his shoulder at the bewildered clerk.

'You figure it out,' he drawled. 'Just make sure you bring me that wine in the next five minutes. I'm thirsty, and when I get thirsty I get real mean. You wouldn't like to see me when I'm mean.'

CHAPTER EIGHT

The snorting mule came trotting into the outskirts of War Smoke with its rider desperately hanging on to the crude reins. Heck Longfellow had to use every scrap of his strength just to keep the stubborn animal heading in the direction he wanted. As he managed to straighten up on his saddle Heck noticed the familiar figure of his fellow deputy staggering out through the swing doors of the Longhorn saloon.

Heck dragged back on his reins. The mule stopped far faster than the special deputy had imagined possible and was sent cartwheeling over the neck and head of his mount. As he hit the ground he saw Elmer weaving his way between a few horses tethered to the saloon's hitching pole. The young deputy stood above Heck and started to chuckle out loud.

'What you doing, Heck?' he asked as he staggered back and forth like a sailor on the open seas. 'It ain't like you to go chewing on dust.'

Heck spat at the ground and then got to his feet. For a few moments he wasn't sure whether it was

Elmer or his mule made him feel angrier.

'You sure look silly, Heck,' Elmer said.

Heck grabbed his hat off the sand and beat it against his baggy pants leg. His eyes narrowed as they fixed on his fellow deputy.

'At least I ain't the one with my pants buttons wide open,' Heck growled as he grabbed the reins of his surly mule. 'Look at you, boy. Showing your long-johns like that. Do yourself up before somebody sees you.'

Elmer rocked on his heels and looked down.

'I thought it was getting a tad chilly,' he chuckled before starting to do up his buttons. 'How come you're in so much of a hurry, Heck?'

'Come on, Nellie gal,' Heck dusted himself down and started leading the mule along the street in the direction of the marshal's office.

Elmer trailed the older man.

'What you bin doing for Marshal Fallen anyway?' he asked as he rubbed his belly.

Heck shook his head. 'I've bin doin' a sort of scoutin' for him. I've bin his eyes and ears out yonder at Boot Hill, Elmer.'

Even a head filled with the fumes of countless glasses of beer could not stop the youngster from being curious. He staggered alongside Heck and leaned over to look into his friend's face.

'What's up in Boot Hill that's so darned interesting, Heck?' the younger man asked as Heck closed the distance between themselves and Fallen's office. 'What was you looking for up there? The place ain't

68

nothing but a graveyard, and we both know that the folks in there ain't likely to try and escape.'

Heck stopped walking and then looked at the swaying Elmer.

'Me and Matthew got a notion that something mighty strange is going on up there, Elmer boy,' Heck stated firmly. 'There's bin a few things going on that we felt I oughta check out.'

Elmer blinked hard and then exhaled.

'Marshal Fallen never told me anything about it, Heck,' he said.

Heck tapped the side of his nose and looked all around him as though he were searching for eavesdroppers.

'Matthew don't tell you everything, Elmer,' he said with a sharp nod of his head. 'You see, I learned about something going on up in the graveyard, and he was interested. We decided that I should go keep a lookout in case things developed.'

'Did they?' Elmer belched.

'You bet your britches they did,' Heck tugged on his reins and then started walking again. 'I gotta tell Matthew about it so we can figure out our next move.'

'How long have you bin a deputy, Heck?' Elmer sighed.

Heck's eyes sharpened as they stared at the young man.

'A special deputy, you mean,' he corrected.

Elmer laughed out loud as they reached the

boardwalk and stepped up on to the warped wooden planks. They were less than ten feet away from the marshal's office.

'I've bin a deputy for the longest while,' he stated. 'You ain't bin wearing that star for half a day.'

Heck wrapped his reins around a wooden porch upright and tied a firm knot. He adjusted his gunbelt and headed for the office door.

'Matthew trusts me to do things he knows you ain't capable of doing, Elmer,' Heck said as he gripped the brass door handle and entered the office. 'If I was you I'd stop sucking on eggs and start acting like a lawman.'

Elmer shrugged and wandered to Fallen's desk. He plonked down on the chair and stared at the cup of untouched coffee he had made for the marshal hours earlier. Heck turned the lamp wheel. The office grew lighter as he looked around for their superior. Fallen rubbed his head and placed his boots on the floorboards. He looked at Heck through blurred eyes.

'Well, you boys sure woke me up from my brief moment of shuteye,' he growled. 'Thanks a heap.'

Heck rushed to the cot.

'I was right, Matthew,' he said excitedly. 'Somebody showed up just like I figured.'

The statement stirred the marshal out of his dreams and made him stare straight at his newly enlisted deputy. Fallen stood up and looked straight into the grinning Heck.

70

'What?' he asked. 'Somebody actually rode out to the graveyard in the middle of the night?'

Heck gave a powerful nod. 'He surely did, Matthew boy. I was tucked up in the undergrowth when this varmint suddenly appeared like a ghost out of the mist. He come riding a darn tall horse and tied the animal to the fence.'

Elmer leaned over the desk and rested his elbows on the ink blotter as he stared at his rival deputy.

'You don't wanna go listening to old Heck, Marshal Fallen,' he dismissed. 'He's spouting hot air. There ain't no such critter as a ghost who appears out of the mist.'

Fallen raised a hand to silence Elmer and then leaned over Heck and waved a finger at his newly appointed deputy.

'You better be telling me the truth, Heck,' he said sternly. 'I ain't in the mood to be joshed with. Did you actually see somebody up at Boot Hill?'

Heck nodded again and placed his hand across the tin star pinned to his chest. 'I swear that I'm telling you the truth, Matt. A rider come visiting that darn graveyard, just like I said. I wouldn't lie to you.'

Fallen patted Heck's shoulder. 'Of course you wouldn't lie to me.'

Elmer shook his head.

'I wouldn't believe that windbag, Marshal Fallen,' he said with a sniff of his nose. 'Everybody in town knows that Heck tells tall tales.'

Heck furrowed his brow. 'I'll punch you if you

71

keep gabbing, Elmer. You see if I don't.'

Matt Fallen rubbed his jaw as he pondered on the information that Heck had given him. He paced around the office and paused by the window. He screwed up his eyes and stared out into the lantern lit street thoughtfully. Finally the tall lawman rested his knuckles on his gunbelt and looked at each of his deputies in turn. It was obvious that Elmer was a long way from being sober, and Heck seemed adamant as to what he had witnessed.

Fallen walked around the desk and pulled two shotguns off the wall rack. He tossed one of the hefty weapons into the hands of Heck and then picked up a box of cartridges. He shared the shotgun shells with Heck and then looked down at the half asleep Elmer. The marshal winked at Heck and then leaned down and whispered into the youngster's ear: 'Drink your damn coffee, Elmer!'

Without thinking, Elmer lifted the coffee mug and took a mouthful of the cold beverage before he recalled that it was the same cup of coffee he had prepared for Fallen hours earlier. His pained expression amused the older men as they made their way to the office door.

Fallen grabbed his hat and led Heck out into the street. As the tall lawman closed the door behind his broad back he snapped the double-barrelled scatter-gun open and pushed two cartridges into it. He cranked the weapon shut and looked all around the street.

'It's still too damn quiet around here,' he complained as Heck copied his actions and loaded his own shotgun. 'I don't like it when it's this quiet, Heck.'

Heck nodded and moved to his mule. 'I ain't got a clue what you mean but I agree that it is kinda silent.'

Fallen pulled the brim of his hat down and moved to the side of his unexpectedly observant deputy. He rested the barrel of the shotgun on his shoulder, and then fished out a couple of silver dollars from his pants' pocket and handed them to Heck.

'Ride down to the livery, Heck,' he ordered. 'Tell Jed to saddle up that grey gelding for me.'

Heck screwed up his eyes and stared at the lawman.

'What you gonna do, Matthew?' he asked. 'Are you gonna take yourself a ride?'

'Nope, we're gonna take us a ride,' Fallen corrected.

'We are?'

'Yep,' Fallen rubbed his neck. 'But first I'm gonna just wander along Front Street with my eyes peeled for that stranger's tall horse, Heck. By the time I reach the livery, Jed should have that grey saddled and ready. You can wait for me there.'

Heck clambered on to his mule and turned the animal as the marshal stepped down on to the street sand. 'Is we going back up to Boot Hill, Matthew? Well, is we?'

Fallen glanced over his shoulder at his deputy and

nodded his head as he strode through the lantern light.

'Yep, we sure are,' Fallen replied.

Heck's expression looked pained as he steadied his mount and watched the marshal through wrinkled eyes.

'But what in tarnation for, Matt?' Heck wondered as he wrestled with the mule. 'That varmint ain't there no more. He up and left the graveyard before I did.'

'I know that,' Fallen said.

'So how come we're going up to Boot Hill?'

'You got me curious. I reckon I should take a look at them graves for myself, Heck,' Fallen drawled.

The newly appointed deputy polished his prized tin star and then thought about the marshal's words. He shook his head and began mumbling under his breath: 'That's plumb stupid!'

Fallen grinned. 'Why is it stupid, Deputy?'

'Hell, graves is just holes in the ground and they all look exactly the same,' Heck got the mule moving and trotted through the lantern light as the tall marshal strode from one hitching rail to the next in search of the tall horse his friend had told him about.

Marshal Fallen paused for a moment and looked along the moonlit length of Front Street as Heck rode his reluctant mount towards the livery. He rubbed his thumb along his jaw and knew that Heck was right about all graves looking exactly alike – but there was something else nagging at his craw.

CHAPTER NINE

Eerily haunting moonlight reflected off the long shotgun barrel balanced on Fallen's left shoulder as the powerfully built lawman moved steadily down Front Street. He had no way of knowing it, but his every step was being watched by the man in black as he steadily drank his way through his second bottle of wine. The marshal checked each and every horse tied up along the wide thoroughfare, completely unaware that the man he sought was seated behind the hotel window's lace drapes.

Even before he had spotted the tin star pinned to Fallen's large chest, Jonas Ward had surmised that anyone who cast such a large shadow could only be one kind of man: only lawmen ever walked with such confidence. Ward lifted his glass to his lips and downed its red contents. His eyes remained fixed on the sturdy Fallen as he moved from one side of the street to the other checking the horses that had been left unattended outside the various saloons and whore houses.

Fallen had looked up to the second-storey windows dotted along Front Street, but almost half of them had some sort of illumination lighting up their frames. Then the fearless lawman concentrated on the boardwalks to both sides of the street. Even the drunkest of cowhands that staggered from one business to the next knew better than to tangle with the famed Fallen. They just politely touched their hat brims and increased their pace.

The lawman instinctively sensed that the man Heck had seen up at the graveyard was probably trouble. His mind raced as he strode along the creaking boardwalks in a desperate bid to try and find answers to the numerous questions that dogged his mind. Yet the marshal knew that he would only find the answers he sought when he reached Boot Hill.

The grave in front of which Heck said the stranger had stopped held the clue he needed. Matt Fallen resigned himself to the fact that he would probably not discover who the stranger was until he, too, set eyes upon the grave marker himself.

Unbeknown to the fearless lawman, he was still being observed. Jonas Ward emptied the second bottle of wine into his tall glass and then removed his silver cigar case from his pocket as he watched Fallen in the street below. He withdrew one of the cigars, then bit off its tip and placed it between his teeth. Never taking his eyes off the tall marshal in the street, Ward stood up beside the table lamp and sucked in the rising heat from its glass funnel. Smoke filled his lungs as his icy stare looked down from his lofty perch at the lawman as he slowly moved past the Diamond Pin Hotel. Ward sat back down and pulled the cigar from his mouth before exhaling.

'Keep on lookin', Marshal,' he grinned as he lifted the glass and inhaled the scent of the wine. 'You ain't gonna find me down there. You ain't gonna find me at all unless I want you to.'

The amused Jonas Ward was like a cat toying with an unsuspecting mouse as he watched Fallen pass directly below his window. He raised his glass and swallowed every last drop of the wine, then placed it down beside the lamp and the ash tray.

'The famous Matt Fallen is scratching around down there looking for answers to questions he ain't even asked me yet,' he said as he carefully removed a cork from another bottle with his expensive corkscrew. 'When I answer them questions he's gonna be too dead to hear me.'

The cork came free of the bottle neck and was carefully placed down in the ash tray. Ward filled his glass again and then smiled even wider.

'He's bigger than I figured, but that just makes things a whole lot easier. The bigger the target, the harder it is to miss.' He laughed. Ward stared at the tall lawman from his high vantage point, and filled his lungs with cigar smoke again. His eyes closed for a few moments as he savoured the flavour of the expensive Havana. When he opened his eyes Fallen had proceeded a hundred feet along the street in his vain hunt.

The man in black placed the cold glass against his throbbing temple and sighed. For as long as he had lived, he had not been able to rid his head of the constant pain in his skull. There had never been a waking moment when the pain ceased to torment him.

He looked at the red liquid in the glass. It was the only thing that eased the constant pain he suffered, and yet for some strange reason he had never been able to drink enough to become intoxicated. It was as though there was something inside his skull which made the vast volumes of liquor he drank no stronger than a child's soda water.

Ward clenched his fist and pressed his knuckles into his temple. Then the smile returned to his face as he remembered why he was in War Smoke. He pulled the lace drape aside and glared down at the lawman's wide back as Fallen continued towards the distant livery stable.

'Soon you'll find out who them graves are for, Fallen,' Ward snarled. 'Soon I'll learn who else gotta die and be buried up in Boot Hill.'

Ward rubbed his painful brow and lifted his glass as though mocking the lawman.

'You don't know it yet, Fallen, but you're a dead man walking.' He grunted. 'You're gonna pay for what you done.'

As the tall lawman disappeared around the corner

on his way to the fragrant livery stable, Ward slid the
lace drape across and opened the sash window. The
stranger in black pushed his boot out on to the
balcony and followed it. As he straightened up, his
icy glare darted around the quiet settlement as he
unclipped his spurs and tossed them into the dimly
lit hotel room.

With the agility of a mountain cat, Ward crossed
the balcony and stepped over its hip-high wooden
surround. He gripped the top of the safety rail and
leaned across the divide between the hotel and its
neighbour. Within a mere heartbeat Ward was on the
sloped porch overhang and moving through the
moonlight towards the adjacent Red Dog saloon. He
threw himself at the saloon's panelled siding and
then, using its downpipe, scrambled up until he was
on the Red Dog rooftop.

As the lean man in black reached its flat rooftop
he crouched and studied everything below his high
perch. Few men could have moved with such preci-
sion over the array of differing structures, but Ward
found it easy. Back in the eastern cities he had mas-
tered the art of ascending far taller structures than
anything to be found in War Smoke.

It was said that no precious item was safe from the
mysterious man who was always clad in black.
Although the law had never discovered his identity
and probably never would have, Ward had suddenly
left the lucrative eastern seaboard for the Wild West.
The true reason was known only to the man in black.

Yet as the constant pain in his skull increased in its severity, Jonas Ward appeared to be driven by only one motive: revenge.

Ward was on a mission, which so far was known only to himself. He carefully moved behind the Red Dog façade and screwed up his eyes as he checked the unlit Havana. He spat out the chewed tobacco leaves and then placed the cigar butt back between his teeth.

His hands searched for a match as he eyed the ground below him like an eagle looking for its next victim. For a few moments Ward could not find the man that his eyes were searching the moonlit ground for. Then Matt Fallen emerged from the shadows and paced across the wide street towards the towering stable.

'There you are, Fallen,' the man in black growled under his breath. 'You're not next on my list. I'm gonna drive you crazy before it's your turn to die, Marshal. I'll have you running around in circles trying to figure this out before I'm through.'

Ward rubbed the palm of his hand against his brow in a vain attempt to stop the continuous pounding inside his head, and then sighed heavily. He glanced around him at the buildings adjoining the saloon. There was nothing to trouble him. He could get to the ground faster than most men could walk across the street.

Although the man in black knew that he could have dropped to the ground from the hotel balcony far more easily than tackling the route he had chosen, Ward realized that few, if any men looked up to the tops of buildings when searching for those they hunted. The rooftops gave him cover.

Ward's slim fingers located a match in his vest pocket. As he held the match in his hand, he knew that his natural ability to scale and negotiate his way over practically any structure, no matter how large, had always given him an advantage over his foes.

Ward scratched the match down the back of the saloon sign to light it, and shielding its flickering flame, touched the blackened tip of his cigar. He drew the acrid smoke deep into his lungs and savoured its flavour for a few moments before exhaling and blowing out the match. With smoke billowing from his mouth he looked around the façade and glared down at Fallen.

Then he diverted his attention to the funeral parlour. Although he had never set eyes on the building before, it matched perfectly the description he had been given. Its lamp light could be seen behind its numerous drawn drapes. Shafts of light fringed the windows as the undertaker went about his business inside the building. The man in black muttered as he noticed movement behind the window drapes: 'So you're still awake, Sam. That's damn considerate of you. I reckon its time that I paid you a little visit. After all, you've done what I paid you to do, and now it's time for you to die.'

Ward pulled the well chewed, expensive cigar

81

from his lips and then gave a sickening smile at the funeral parlour. He extinguished the cigar by pressing its glowing end into the wooden boards beside his shoulder, and as he crushed the butt he gritted his teeth and wisps of scarlet drifted unseen into the moonlight.

The burning red embers floated unnoticed into the night air like a swarm of fireflies on the wing – but they didn't last very long in the cool temperature that slowly blanketed War Smoke. As the last of them faded into memory, the stranger in black had vanished into the blackness and was continuing towards his goal.

CHAPTER TEN

Moonlight danced across the shotgun resting on the marshal's shoulder as he slowly walked up the slight rise to the livery stable. The tall figure of Matt Fallen sensed that something was wrong in War Smoke and yet he still could not work out what. The years of wearing a tin star had taught Fallen many things, and the biggest of those lessons was that you always trusted your guts.

For a long time Matt Fallen had felt that War Smoke was like a volcano about to erupt. It had happened on many occasions during his time as a marshal, and he imagined that it would continue to do so for as long as the vast settlement continued to exist. All that men like Fallen could ever do was to ride the rampaging fortunes of fate and hope that they survived the tempestuous trouble when it eventually raised its head.

Fallen eyed the area as he approached the livery stable and walked towards the distinctive mule tethered to the coral fencing. The lawman lowered the hefty scattergun off his shoulder and strode along the fragrant wooden structure. He paused beside the mule and patted the animal as his eyes searched the shadows which surrounded him. The relative calm was shattered within seconds as Heck came rushing out of the livery like a squirrel with its tail on fire.

'Matthew,' Heck repeatedly called out to the towering figure as he ran with his left hand holding up his oversized pants.

Fallen shook his head. 'Easy, Heck. You don't wanna bust nothing. Calm down.'

Heck stopped beside Fallen and rested a hand on the far taller man to steady himself as he caught his breath.

'There you are, Matthew,' he gasped. 'I just found that real tall horse I was telling you about.'

Fallen narrowed his eyes.

'It's in the livery?' he asked in surprise.

Heck nodded and caught his battered old hat in his hands before returning it to his head of wayward hair.

'It sure is,' he replied. 'As big as life. I asked Jed who it belongs to but all he could say was that it belongs to a stranger.'

Fallen raised his eyebrows. 'We figured that already, Heck. The thing is, what's the name of the stranger?'

Heck looked bemused.

'Jed didn't get no name, Matthew,' he explained. 'All he could tell me was the fella that owns that nag was dressed all in black.'

Marshal Fallen tilted his head as a chilling thought came to him. He leaned closer to Heck.

'Like an undertaker?' he asked.

Heck's eyes widened.

'Yeah, like an undertaker.' He nodded nervously. 'I never thought about that, Matthew. Just like an undertaker dresses. Goddamn.'

Fallen exhaled and rubbed his chin with his knuckles.

'Is that gelded grey ready?' he asked his deputy.

Heck was still nodding. 'Yep, I'll go fetch it for you.'

The marshal paced out into the middle of the rough track leading into the livery stable as Heck vanished into the building. Fallen glanced around the structures that flanked the tall livery, searching for a glimpse of the mysterious stranger he had just been informed about. But just as he had assumed, the man in black was long gone. The sound of the horse's hoofs drew his attention to the wide open barn doors, and he turned as Heck appeared in the moonlight leading the saddle horse.

Fallen walked over to his deputy and took the long reins; he grabbed the saddle horn, poked his left boot into the stirrup and mounted the animal. Still deep in thought, he gathered up his reins as he watched Heck clamber up on to the mule and quickly turn the animal.

'Did Jed happen to mention where that *hombre* went after leaving his tall-shouldered stallion here, Heck?' he asked the dishevelled deputy.

'Jed told him about the Diamond Pin, Matthew,' Heck replied as he adjusted his gun belt. 'I reckon he must be there. Why?'

Fallen tapped the sides of the grey and allowed the horse to walk to the side of the mule.

'The Diamond Pin, huh?' Fallen nodded. 'We'll go check to see if he's there later, Heck.'

Heck shrugged. 'This is gonna be a long night.'

'They always are, Heck,' Fallen spurred his horse into a trot, leaving a cloud of dust in its wake. 'You'll find that out if you pass your deputy exams.'

Heck Longfellow jerked his reins and slapped the mule's tail. The mule responded to its master's encouragement and trotted until it had drawn level with the grey. Heck held on to his hat and looked up into Fallen's emotionless face.

'What does them deputy exams entail exactly, Matthew?' he asked as the animals headed out of War Smoke and on towards Boot Hill.

'Nothing too difficult, Heck,' Fallen grinned and stood up in his stirrups. 'If you don't get killed before sun-up, I reckon you'll pass.' Heck squinted at the moonlit hill of grave stones and markers they were approaching as he pondered on the marshal's words.

'What if I gets myself just wounded?' he shouted at

the broad back of the sturdy marshal. 'Would I pass then?'

Fallen did not bother to respond.

CHAPTER ELEVEN

The wall clock inside the marshal's office chimed loudly to mark the passing of another hour. Elmer lifted his head off the ink blotter and turned to stare at the clock. By the time his eyes had managed to focus, the deafening noise had stopped. The deputy rested the palms of his hands on the desk and forced himself upright on Fallen's chair. He rubbed the sleep from his eyes and squinted hard at the clock.

'Two o'clock,' he mumbled to himself, and wondered why his mouth tasted like nothing he could recall either eating or drinking. 'What happened to midnight?'

Elmer gingerly got to his feet and exhaled. His head was filled with a painful reminder of the countless drinks he had happily consumed vainly chasing the Longhorn saloon's latest employee.

The deputy walked to the window and looked out over its lower blind. The street was quiet, but at least two of its saloons and gambling houses spilled their glowing light out on to the moonlit sand. Elmer rubbed his head and blinked hard as his attention was drawn to the rifle rack beside the wall clock.

'Now that's odd,' he drawled as he moved across the office and touched the rack with his fingertips. 'By my figuring, there happens to be two scatterguns missing.'

He checked the chain which was usually threaded through the hand and trigger guards of the individual weapons. Its padlock was unlocked and resting on the rack.

'Marshal Fallen must have taken the scatterguns,' he told himself as he moved around the desk and picked up the tin cup he had emptied of its contents earlier, and moved toward the flat-topped stove where the coffee pot rested. He grabbed a cloth and then filled the cup with the remnants of the pot before pondering. 'But why would he take two scatterguns?'

The bemused deputy rested his lean hip on the edge of the desk as he blew the steam off his beverage. His mind was still trying to work out how he had ended up in the office when the last thing he could remember was being in the Longhorn.

He sipped the black brew. Luckily for Elmer he was still too hung over to be able to taste what he was swallowing. Then he remembered vaguely talking to Heck Longfellow. He finished the strong coffee and rested the cup on a pile of Wanted posters, and rubbed his aching features with his hands. He forced his weary body to the door and opened it, and the cool night air hit him hard. He staggered to the water trough and rested a hand on the pump, staring at his reflection in the coffin of water.

'I sure hope I don't look as bad as that fella,' he quipped before splashing the cold water over his face and neck. He sat on the edge of the trough as droplets of water dripped from his soaked face. His mind was still filled with fog, which was only just beginning to clear.

'What in tarnation was Heck doing with Marshal Fallen?' he muttered – then remembered the tin star pinned to Heck's chest. He snapped his fingers. 'I remember! The marshal hired Heck as a special deputy. Holy buttermilk, I might be getting replaced by a man who uses rope to hold up his pants.'

Elmer stood up and tapped his lips with his fingers, his mind in a whirl. A bead of sweat trailed down the side of his face and dripped on to his shirt as he wondered if Marshal Fallen was about to fire him. He thought about the two missing shotguns, and then slowly started to make sense of the missing hours. He rested a hand on the porch upright and steadied his lurching frame for a few moments.

'Heck and the marshal must have gone some-place,' he reasoned as he stepped back up on to the boardwalk and entered the office again. 'They must have figured it might be dangerous and that's why they up and took the scatterguns. Marshal Fallen must have bin plumb disappointed in me not being able to go with him. I'd best pull my socks up if'n I wanna keep my job.'

Without hesitating, Elmer moved to the rack and pulled down a Winchester, and checked its magazine. The weapon was fully loaded and primed for action. He pulled the handguard back up, and started for the door. As the lean, long-legged youngster stepped back out into the night air he narrowed his eyes. He closed the office door and moved back towards the moonlight.

'I'll show Heck what a real deputy does to earn his wages, by thunder,' Elmer muttered, stepping down on to the sand and walking down the centre of the wide empty street. 'Heck ain't gonna get my job without a tussle. I ain't always drunk.'

With no notion of where he was going or why he was going there, Elmer decided he should pace the streets of War Smoke, just as he and Fallen had been doing for years. With the repeating rifle firmly gripped in his hands, the young deputy slowly started to retrace the route he and his superior always took when checking the hundreds of buildings in the sprawling settlement.

CHAPTER TWELVE

Bathed in moonlight and covered in mist, Boot Hill resembled something from the depths of their worst nightmares – but the riders continued on up the grassy slope towards it regardless. The large moon cast its brilliant illumination over the countless stones and wooden markers that practically covered the expanse of hillside set aside as War Smoke's graveyard. Matt Fallen eased back on his reins as his saddle horse neared the white picket fencing that surrounded the cemetery. Suddenly it shied, and the marshal had to tap his spurs into its flanks to keep it moving forwards.

The grey gelding snorted its disapproval and slowed to a walk before the lawman stopped it. Fallen stared at the unholy sight before him with cold, calculating eyes. He knew that he was responsible for at least a third of the bodies buried here. A haunting mist hung over the many markers and headstones as night progressed on its course towards its inevitable journey to sunrise.

Heck pulled back on his crude reins and stopped his mule beside the lawman. The older man rubbed his face and rested his wrists on his saddle horn.

'Ain't a pretty sight, is it?' Heck chirped as he clambered off the back of the mule and tied its reins to the fence posts.

'Nope, it ain't pretty, Heck,' Fallen agreed as he swung his leg over the saddle cantle and lowered his huge frame to the ground. The tall figure of the marshal held his long reins firmly, his eyes narrowed. Heck rubbed his whiskers and swallowed hard. After Fallen had secured his reins to the fence, both men walked through the gap in it – a gap just wide enough to allow access for Sam Foster's glass-sided hearse.

'I still don't quite understand what we're doing here, Matthew,' Heck ventured as he nervously walked beside the lofty lawman. 'That varmint in black ain't here no longer. His nag is in Jed's livery and he's more than likely holed up in a nice warm bed in the Diamond Pin.'

Fallen stopped walking.

'I know that,' he sighed as he surveyed the numerous markers facing them. 'I ain't looking for him, I'm looking for what he was looking at, Heck.'

Totally bemused, Heck held on to his gunbelt and squared up to the far taller man. 'Say that again, 'coz I didn't savvy one word of it.'

Fallen's honed senses could hear the wildlife in

the mass of trees beyond the boundary of the cemetery. Then he stared at the cold mist lingering a few
feet above the cold ground. He turned to his pal.

'Where are the freshly dug graves, Heck?' he
asked. 'I can't see them.'

Heck nervously pointed a shaking arm to the
darkest part of the graveyard.

'They're over yonder.'

Matt Fallen strode carefully between the markers
to where his deputy had indicated. The overhanging
tree branches from the woodland behind the cemetery prevented the bright moonlight from reaching
the three deep holes. Fallen stepped over one of the
mounds of soil and then rested his hands on his hips
and studied them.

'They're deep enough,' he commented.

'They surely are, Matthew,' Heck agreed as his
head twisted on its neck. 'You could stack about
three coffins in each of them if'n you wanted.'

Fallen rubbed his neck thoughtfully.

'Damned if I can figure who would pay for this,' he
muttered at the deep holes. 'You said that old Sam
got a fifty dollar bill in the mail to have these graves
dug, Heck?'

'That's what Sam told me,' the special deputy
nodded.

'If it's a joke it's a real expensive one.' Fallen muttered.

Heck was only a few steps behind the marshal. He
looked from around Fallen's left elbow at the empty

graves. Sweat defied the dropping temperature and rolled freely down his face.

'A mite creepy, ain't it?' Heck said in a hushed voice as his eyes darted around the shadows.

Marshal Fallen looked down at his trembling deputy and raised an eyebrow.

'What's creepy about three holes in the ground, Heck?' he asked. 'It seems to me that someone's planning to kill three folks, and this is a warning.'

'Well ain't that just dandy.' Heck remarked at his superior's statement. 'You sure know how to unsettle a critter, Matthew.'

'Relax,' Fallen said calmly. 'Save your fretting until the shooting starts.'

Heck looked over both shoulders and then back up into the face of his towering friend. He stretched his neck and stood on tiptoe.

'Boot Hill is spooky enough at the best of times but with three fresh dug holes and nobody to fill them up, it just seems worse!' He hissed quietly.

'Why are you whispering, Heck?' Fallen asked and waved his arms around at the surrounding area. 'You ain't gonna wake anyone up around here even if you yelled your lungs out.'

Heck considered the marshal's words for a while, but before he could respond Fallen spoke again.

'You said that this *hombre* in black walked to a marker and kinda lingered there for a while, Heck,' he stated. 'Which marker did he go and look at?'

Heck scratched his chin and then pointed to their

right and jabbed his finger at the air.

'He went over there, Matthew,' he replied.

Matt Fallen nodded and headed to where his recently appointed deputy was indicating. After a handful of steps between the headstones and markers he reached the wooden marker board and studied it. Then something caught the attention of the marshal. He gazed down at the muddy ground and the two boot prints that were pointed at the grave marker.

Fallen knew that the stranger in black had left the clear impressions in the soft damp mud as he had spent a few moments looking at the wooden marker.

'That's the one,' Heck said pointing at the wooden rectangle placed at the head of the grave. 'That *hombre* was plumb interested in it.'

The marshal ran a thumbnail along his powerful jaw.

'I know,' Fallen said as his narrowed eyes stared at the hastily painted name and date on the board. 'He left his boot prints here.'

Heck moved to the side of the lawman and squinted at the marker and its hastily painted lettering. 'Is them words?'

'Sure they're words,' Fallen grunted. 'Can't you read?'

'Nope,' Heck readily admitted. 'It looks like a bunch of Chinese to me.'

The marshal patted his deputy on the back.

'Oh yeah, I forgot,' Fallen looked at the name on

the crude marker. He nodded confidently. 'Now this is all starting to make sense, Heck.'

No matter how hard Heck stared at the grave marker it was still nothing but strange splashes of paint to him. He shook his head in frustration.

'Who in tarnation is buried there, Matthew?' he asked.

Fallen turned and started back across the grave-yard to where they had left their mounts. Heck scurried after the marshal like a puppy trying to get its master's attention.

Fallen pulled his long reins loose of the fence posts and turned the grey horse. He stood like a statue as his eyes thoughtfully stared down at War Smoke and its array of amber lights.

'I figured that hanging and planting that *hombre* up here would be the end of it,' he sighed. 'Looks like I was wrong, Heck.'

Heck stood between the marshal and the distant settlement until Fallen finally looked at him.

'Who is buried over yonder, Matthew?' he asked for the second time. 'I'm kinda curious.'

Fallen grabbed his saddle horn, then stepped into his stirrup and hoisted himself up on to the back of the skittish grey animal. As the marshal held his horse firmly in check he looked down at his deputy. 'Have you ever heard of a varmint named Lucas Ward, Heck?'

Heck raised his eyebrows as his mind raced. He pulled his crude reins free of the white picket fence and then climbed up on to the saddle of his mule.

'Lucas Ward?' he repeated the name and then shook his head. 'Nope, I can't rightly say that I do recall anyone named Lucas Ward, Matthew. Who the hell is he?'

'He was a cold-blooded killer,' Fallen sighed heavily. 'A loco-bean that took sordid pleasure from killing innocents just for the pleasure it gave him.'

'When was this, Matthew?' Heck squinted.

Fallen moved his horse next to the mule and rested a wrist on his saddle pommel. 'It was close to a year back.'

'I was off in the high country fur trapping back then,' Heck remembered. 'I didn't get back here until about three or four months ago.'

Marshal Fallen winked at his deputy and tapped his boots against the flanks of the grey. Both riders started to steer their mounts back towards War Smoke.

'He was a mindless killer, Heck,' he explained. 'I caught him standing over his last victim with a bloody knife in his hand. Lucas Ward was totally insane, but he was also a coward and gave up without a fight. He rested in one of my cells for a few weeks until the jury found him guilty and the district judge sentenced him to hang.'

'Well ain't that just the way,' Heck shook his head. 'There ain't bin a hanging in War Smoke for years and when there is one, I miss it. Damn, I enjoy a good hanging.'

Fallen narrowed his eyes as he continued to steer his mount towards the glowing lights of the sprawling settlement.

Heck looked back at Boot Hill and then at Fallen.

'Why didn't you just shoot the bastard, Matthew?' he asked. 'It seems to me that if'n you catch a critter standing over his last victim with a smoking .45 in his hand, you just shoot him.'

Fallen nodded.

'Ward dropped his knife as soon as he spotted me and Elmer so we couldn't just kill him,' he said. 'Anyway, when we had him locked up he kept writing letters to his brother back east. I don't know what he wrote exactly but he began to actually believe that he was innocent and we'd made the whole thing up.'

Heck adjusted his holster. 'He sure sounds like a real loco-bean to me, Matthew.'

Matt Fallen smiled.

'The name his letters were addressed to was a certain Jonas Ward,' the marshal remembered as they drew closer to the large settlement. 'I've got me a feeling chewing at my craw that's the *hombre* we've bin looking for, Heck.'

Heck Longfellow polished his deputy star with his cuff and stared blankly ahead. He felt no safer by knowing the probable identity of the mysterious man in black.

'I still reckon you should have shot the critter when you caught him, Matthew,' he muttered. 'For

all we know his brother is as crazy as he was.'
   'You might be right,' Fallen nodded.

CHAPTER THIRTEEN

The cool night air had sobered up the deputy as he rounded the corner and headed back into Front Street again. He held the Winchester in his left hand as he crossed from the café towards the funeral parlour. Elmer had circled War Smoke just as he and Matt Fallen had done on countless previous occasions, and was surprised that the town was even quieter than usual.

As he reached the Rolling Dice gambling hall his attention was drawn to the muted sound of laughter coming from behind its locked doors. Elmer smiled to himself and glanced up along the porched board-walk. Neither the bright moon nor the street lantern light was capable of illuminating the boardwalk under the various overhangs, yet Elmer spotted something which he thought was unusual.

The unmistakable figure of Sam Foster was seated directly in front of one of the funeral parlour windows. Elmer grinned as he hastened his approach.

'What you doing out here, Sam?' he called out. 'It's too damn cold to be outside. You'll catch your death.'

There was no response to the deputy's words from the seated undertaker. Elmer slowed his pace as he got closer to the old man. Sam was sitting dressed in his business finery with his chin resting on his chest. The undertaker gave the impression that he was asleep, but the hairs on Elmer's neck started to tingle.

'Sam?' Elmer repeated over and over as he reached the motionless figure.

No matter how much the deputy raised his voice, the seated man did not respond or move. Elmer cautiously rested his rifle against the wall of the building and reluctantly touched the bald-headed figure.

'Wake up, Sam,' Elmer croaked. 'Wake up!'

But Sam Foster would never awaken. He was no longer residing in the thin body which he had occupied for so many decades. Elmer pressed his fingers into the neck of the undertaker in a fashion that he had seen Doc Weaver do many times before.

There was no pulse.

Elmer straightened up.

A chill washed over the young deputy. The reality of what he had discovered finally dawned on him as he rested his back against the wall of the funeral parlour. His heart was pounding in shock. Then his attention was drawn to the sound of hoofs at the far end of the street. Elmer glanced up and saw the two familiar figures of the marshal and Heck riding slowly towards the livery. He rushed to the edge of the boardwalk and waved his arms frantically at them.

'Marshal Fallen!' he bellowed.

Recognizing the voice of his distressed deputy, Matt Fallen halted the grey and swung the animal around until he caught sight of his deputy. It was quite obvious to the seasoned lawman that Elmer was far more upset than he had ever seen him be before. Fallen indicated to Heck and then galloped to the funeral parlour. Both the gelded grey and the mule covered the distance quickly.

They hauled rein.

'What's wrong, Elmer?' Fallen asked, taking note of the ashen expression on Elmer's face. He steadied the grey, and then spotted the lifeless form of the undertaker behind his deputy. He quickly dismounted, stepped up on to the boardwalk and dropped on to one knee beside the stricken old man. He looked up at Heck who was steadying his mule, and indicated to his special deputy to turn around:

'Go wake Doc up, Heck,' he ordered. 'Drag him out of bed if you have to, but get him here fast. Tell him that I think Sam is dead but I need him to confirm it.'

'Right away, Matthew,' Heck pulled his reins hard to his right and then slapped his mule's tail. The cantankerous animal galloped down Front Street.

Fallen returned to his full height and removed his Stetson to mop his brow on his shirt sleeve. He looked at the shocked Elmer and patted the youngster on the back.

'Steady, boy,' he said.

'Is old Sam dead, Marshal Fallen?' the deputy stammered. 'Is he?'

Fallen returned his hat to his head and thoughtfully rubbed his jaw as he stared down at the undertaker. Sam was dressed in his best funeral attire and sat with his bald head lowered. Both lawmen had seen him like this many times before, but this time it was very different.

'I think so, Elmer,' he drawled. 'Doc will have to confirm it though.'

'Glory be,' Elmer shook his head. He had seen numerous people dead before, but this time he was visibly shaken. He moved to the side of the marshal. 'The poor old galoot must have fallen asleep and then just quit living.'

'Sam was mighty old, Elmer,' Fallen sighed. 'Most folks don't live long enough to get as old as he did.'

'Fancy coming out here to sit down and then die, Marshal Fallen,' Elmer muttered. 'I guess Sam was old, but it just don't seem right to up and die like this.'

Fallen nodded.

'We all got to die sometime, Elmer,' he said as he moved back to the seated body. 'I reckon that it was his time. Sam was old. Hell, he was old when I first

104

came to War Smoke.'

Elmer watched the marshal step back to where Sam was seated.

'What you figuring on doing, Marshal Fallen?'

'I'm gonna take him inside, Elmer,' Fallen answered.

'I'll help you,' Elmer said.

Fallen shook his head.

'There ain't no need, Elmer boy.' The marshal patted his young friend's arm. 'Sam don't weigh much more than a sack of feathers. I can handle him easy enough.'

Elmer watched as the marshal carefully slid his arms under the shoulders and legs of the undertaker. Fallen straightened up and moved to the slightly ajar door. The deputy trailed his superior into the office as the marshal laid Sam on the long counter.

'I'll turn up the lights,' the deputy said as he hurriedly turned the brass wheels of the parlour's lamps until the room was bathed in amber light. Then the deputy stared at the undertaker's face and sighed. 'I reckon it must have bin old age or the like, Marshal Fallen.'

There was no response from Fallen as the far bigger lawman walked towards one of the closest lamps. Elmer glanced at Fallen who had his back to him.

'What's wrong, Marshal Fallen?' he asked.

'It wasn't old age that killed Sam, Elmer,' Fallen said as he slowly turned to face the deputy. Elmer's eyes widened as they saw the blood on the marshal's hands as Fallen continued to look at his crimson palms. He then watched as the tall lawman inspected the body more carefully in the bright room.

'You mean Sam was shot?' he gulped.

'Not shot, Elmer,' Fallen corrected before looking into his deputy's face. 'Sam was brutally stabbed.'

'Stabbed?'

'Yep, stabbed,' Fallen nodded, wiping his hands on the legs of his pants, then walked back out into the street. The seasoned lawman rested a hand on the wooden upright and shook his head in disbelief.

Why would anyone kill old Sam? The question tormented him as he heard the echoing of hoofs. Fallen looked up and saw Heck riding through the moonlight towards him. He moved to the hitching rail as Heck dropped to the sand and rushed excitedly towards him.

'Doc's on his way, Matthew,' Heck blustered.

Fallen nodded and then turned on his heels and looked into the funeral parlour at Elmer.

'Stay here and help Doc, Elmer,' he ordered, then stepped down beside the grey gelding. He pulled the shotgun from its saddle scabbard and then gestured to Heck. 'You come with me.'

'Where we going, Matthew?' the special deputy asked as Fallen strode past him and started to cross the street.

Fallen tossed the shotgun into Heck's hands and

then flicked the safety loop off his holstered six-shooter. He glanced over his wide shoulder at the pal.

'We're going to the Diamond Pin Hotel, Heck,' he snarled, his long stride beginning to increase in pace. 'I'm gonna check to see if Jonas Ward is registered there.'

'You gonna arrest him, Matthew?' Heck asked.

Fallen gritted his teeth.

'Nope, if he's got one speck of blood on him I'm gonna kill him, Heck.' He snarled.

CHAPTER FOURTEEN

Heck had to practically run just to keep up with the determined marshal as they reached the opposite boardwalk and proceeded towards the hotel. Puffing and panting like an old hound dog after a ten-mile run, Heck managed to get level with Fallen.

'What if that varmint is as wily as his dead brother was, Matthew?' Heck nervously asked. 'He might be loco enough to prefer a rope to a fight.'

'I ain't making the same mistake that I made last time, Heck,' Fallen stepped down from one wooden walkway, crossed a stretch of sand and then stepped up on to another boardwalk. 'If I'd have shot Lucas and not arrested him he wouldn't have written to his brother. Sam would still be alive.'

'If this varmint actually killed Sam,' Heck said.

'My guts tell me that this varmint killed Sam, Heck,' Fallen snarled. 'And if he did, I'll kill him.'

Both men reached the Diamond Pin and headed for its double doors. Fallen pushed them apart with his left hand and marched across the foyer towards the desk. The clerk saw the two tin stars approaching, and nervously rose to his feet.

'What can I do for you, Marshal?' he asked as Fallen and Heck reached the desk.

Without uttering a word, Fallen grabbed the register and swung the open book round until it faced him. Heck squinted at the page as Fallen ran his finger down the various scribblings until he reached the name he sought. He jabbed the page with his finger.

'There he is,' he said.

The small clerk looked at the signature and then at Fallen, and raised his eyebrows. He could not believe that the lawman was confident as to the name of the hotel guest.

'You can read that?' he asked.

'Matthew can read it, sonny,' Heck sniffed and looked up at his tall friend. 'You can read it, can't you?'

Matt Fallen looked long and hard at the hotel clerk.

'Was the *hombre* who wrote that clad all in black?' he asked the nervous man behind the desk.

'He sure was,' the timid clerk nodded. 'That fella was dressed from head to toe in black. He bought every bottle of wine, and I took it up to his room. A real weird cuss.'

'Wine?' Fallen raised his eyebrows.

The clerk nodded. 'Yep, wine.'

Heck screwed up his face and rested the barrel of his scattergun on the desk.

'Was he armed?' he asked.

The clerk nodded nervously and pointed at the shotgun. 'He didn't have one of those. He did have a six-shooter, though.'

'He had himself a hog-leg, Matthew,' Heck repeated to Fallen.

The clerk mopped his face with a handkerchief. 'He had himself a real fancy six-shooter that looked like silver or something akin to it.'

'That don't fill me with courage, Matthew,' Heck told his tall companion as he yawned. 'In fact it kinda makes me feel damn troubled.'

The clerk looked faint and sat back down. He loosened his collar and tried to stop his legs from shaking, but it was a pointless exercise.

'There ain't gonna be a lot of blood again, is there, Marshal?' he croaked, watching as the two star-packing men moved towards the staircase. 'The last time we had trouble at the Diamond Pin it took a week to get the blood off the walls.'

Matt Fallen glanced back at the terrified desk clerk trembling on his stool.

'Then stop painting the damn place white,' he suggested. 'You're just asking for problems.'

Both law officers started the long ascent up the newly laid stair carpet. The thick pile absorbed the sound of their heavy boots.

'Where we headed?' Heck asked clutching the shotgun to his chest beside the marshal. The older lawman was tired and visibly in need of sleep as they both studied the gas lights dotted around them.

'Room three,' Fallen growled as his hand slid his six-shooter out of its holster and his thumb pulled back on its hammer until it fully locked. 'That's the room that Jonas Ward is meant to be in, Heck.'

They reached the ornately decorated landing and glanced down the quiet corridors which led off in three separate directions. All the gas wall lights had been dimmed, but Fallen's keen eyes quickly spotted the room they were looking for. He pointed the barrel of his .45 and Heck nodded.

The years of wearing a tin star had taught Matt Fallen the art of caution and surprise, and he intended to use both qualities to his advantage. The pair of lawmen moved stealthily along the corridor with their weapons aimed at the door with the number three painted upon its polished surface. Not a sound came from the hotel room, but the famed marshal was well aware that that meant nothing when it was a question of confronting a certain breed of man.

This might be a trap, he deduced, and there was no way he was going to be caught out like old Sam had been. If Jonas Ward was the killer they sought, he would not catch Fallen in such a trap.

The lawmen made their way halfway along the corridor until they reached the rooms that faced Front

Street. Matt Fallen pressed a finger against his lips to signal his partner to remain silent. Then he gestured for Heck to move to one side of the room door while he remained at the other. The scruffy deputy clutched the hefty shotgun in readiness and watched as the muscular marshal raised his left boot.

When his knee was touching his chest, Fallen steadied himself for a few moments. Summoning every ounce of his tremendous strength he forcefully kicked the brass door handle.

The entire hotel resounded to the mighty kick as Fallen's boot leather collided with the door. Its lock shattered into a thousand metal fragments as the door splintered inwards and fell from its frame. A cloud of sawdust hung in the lamplight as Fallen charged into the room with his six-gun drawn in readiness.

CHAPTER FIFTEEN

No sooner had the last fragment of the door and its frame fallen to the floor than the determined lawman came to an abrupt halt beside the small table near the window. Ward's holstered six-shooter lay near a glowing lamp. The crouching Fallen swung on his boots with his gun clutched in his hand in search of the stranger. A mere beat of his pounding heart later and he spotted the man in black resting upon the bed in the corner.

Jonas Ward was smiling as he lay against his stacked pillows with an empty bottle in one hand and a full glass in the other. He downed the contents of the glass and then placed both vessels on the bed to either side of him.

Fallen aimed his cocked .45 at Ward.

'Don't move or I'll shoot, Ward,' he warned.

'I'm unarmed, Marshal,' the man in black said as he held his hands high. 'My six-shooter is over near the window.'

Fallen could not help but be impressed by the sheer confidence in Ward. 'You might have another weapon hidden in that long black coat you're wearing. I ain't the sort to take risks.'

Ward smiled. 'I've no hidden weapons, Marshal.'

'That's a shame,' Fallen said as he slowly straightened up. 'I was hoping to kill the man that just stabbed the town undertaker.'

'It wasn't me, Marshal,' he said in a hushed tone.

'I've only got your word for that,' Matt Fallen surveyed the hotel room. He had expected to be greeted by a plague of bullets and not a mocking grin. The lamp bathed the entire room in its amber light and glistened off the empty wine bottles scattered across the floor. The lawman trained his .45 at the seemingly tired man. He was not in any mood to be friendly with a man he did not trust.

'Get to your feet, Ward,' Fallen snarled as Heck nervously followed him into the room. Ward slowly rolled over until his feet found the floorboards. He glanced at the tall marshal and smiled ominously at him.

'I'm impressed that you managed to work out who I am, Marshal,' he sighed before adding. 'But I haven't done a thing to warrant you kicking in my hotel room door.'

'Search this *hombre*, Heck,' Fallen instructed his deputy.

Ward stood and swayed as he kept his hands held above his head. Heck had his shotgun under his arm and patted down the seemingly drunk stranger. When Heck was finished he stepped back and held his hefty double-barrelled weapon. He kept it aimed at Ward.

'He ain't got no weapons on him, Matthew,' the deputy looked disappointed. 'I looked real hard for a knife but he ain't got one.'

Fallen could feel his rage fermenting as he took a step towards the man in black and pushed him back on to the bed.

'I know that you killed Sam Foster, Ward,' the marshal said as he somehow managed to control his temper.

'Who is Sam Foster?' Ward asked as he stared through half-closed eyes. 'I've never heard of anyone by that name.'

'He was the undertaker, Ward,' Fallen snarled. 'You gutted an innocent old man who never harmed anyone in his whole life, and I'll make sure you hang for that.'

Ward sighed as he sat on the edge of the bed. He then looked up at the fuming lawman and his expression changed. The smile had been replaced by an icy glare.

'Not me, Marshal,' he hissed through gritted teeth. 'I've bin in this room ever since I registered. Why would I kill the undertaker? I've never even set foot in War Smoke before tonight and I sure ain't ever met your friend, so what reason would I have to kill him?'

'He's lying, Matthew,' Heck growled as his finger stroked the triggers of the scattergun. 'That critter is as guilty as sin. He's full of hogwash.'

'I'm totally innocent, Marshal,' Ward repeated his claim. 'You're confusing me with my brother.'

The statement was a valid one. There did not seem to be any reason why the man in black would kill someone that he had never met before. Yet Fallen was positive that he was looking at the killer as he paced around the room. He kicked the empty bottles out of his path and came to a halt beside the bed. He looked down at the seated man.

'You've never bin to War Smoke before?' Fallen repeated the statement.

Jonas Ward shrugged.

'Nope, this is the first time, Marshal,' Ward said as he leaned forward and stared at the floorboards. 'Reckon I won't be coming back here either.'

'Why not?' the marshal wondered.

Ward sighed. 'It's hard to get a decent bottle of wine here. I'll be glad to get back to civilization.'

'You sure drunk enough of it though,' Heck scratched his beard as he kept his twin-barrelled weapon aimed at Ward. 'I ain't ever seen so many empty bottles in one place before.'

Matt Fallen tilted his head as he stared down at the man in his gun sights. He pointed at the array of bottles scattered between the bed and the small table.

'Are you telling me that you drunk all this wine,

116

Ward?' he asked the yawning man. 'Are you?'

Ward nodded and frowned.

'That's what I'm telling you, Marshal.'

Heck moved closer to the marshal. 'That's a heap of wine to drink on your lonesome, Matthew. Most folks would be unable to walk if they only drunk half that much.'

Fallen narrowed his eyes and looked down upon the stranger in black. Was Jonas Ward actually drunk or was he just pretending?

'Get up, Ward,' he demanded.

After what appeared to be some considerable effort, Ward managed to stand but then within seconds he fell back on to the bed.

Heck moved closer to Fallen.

'This *hombre* can't be the fella that killed old Sam, Matthew,' he said shaking his head. 'Somehow we've taken the wrong trail. We've bin chasing the wrong fox.'

Still unable to accept that he had made a mistake, Fallen grabbed Ward's collar with his free hand and then pressed the cold barrel of his six-shooter into the man's neck.

'I'm gonna check to find out if you've sneaked out of this room tonight, Ward,' he growled before releasing his grip. 'If I find out you've bin lying to me, I'll be back with my guns blazing. Savvy?'

'I savvy, Marshal,' Ward sighed before rubbing his throbbing temple.

'How come you drunk so much wine, boy?' Heck

117

asked as he stared down the double barrels of his shotgun. 'That seems like an awful lot of hooch for a man to drink on his lonesome.'

Ward shrugged. 'Maybe it is a lot but I was thirsty. You see, it was a long dry train ride here and once I'd put my horse in the livery I came straight here. The desk clerk sold me the wine and I drank every damn drop of it.'

'He's lying,' Heck shook his head at Ward's statement. 'He didn't come straight here, Matthew. I seen him up at Boot Hill.'

'Yeah, that's right you did, Heck.' Fallen nodded before looking back at the seated Ward. 'You took a little ride up to the graveyard before you went to the livery and rented this room.'

'I forgot. I did ride up to the graveyard,' Ward admitted with a shrug. 'I wanted to see where my brother was laid to rest. That's not a crime is it?'

Matt Fallen continued to stare at Ward. Every sinew in his body told him that he was being lied to and yet he could not prove it. Jonas Ward looked a lot like his dead brother but that was where the similarity ended. Lucas had been stupid. Jonas was smart and devious.

'How come you was looking at them three fresh dug graves?' Heck snorted at Ward. 'That's kinda fishy if'n you ask me.'

Jonas Ward nodded.

'I was wondering why there were three empty graves up there myself,' he taunted the bearded

118

deputy. 'I agree that's mighty strange.'

Matt Fallen realized that his only suspect seemed to have an alibi. He indicated to his deputy and then nodded to the man seated on the edge of the bed. 'We're sorry to have disturbed you, Ward. Reckon we made a mistake.'

Before Heck could continue arguing with the mysterious stranger, Fallen's large hands had hustled him out of the room and back into the corridor. The tall lawman slid his gun back into its holster and rubbed his jaw.

'That *hombre* is lying, Matthew,' Heck said as Fallen led him back to the top of the staircase. 'I can feel it in my bones. He's our man. He killed Sam.'

'I know he did,' Fallen agreed as they started down to the foyer. 'The thing is I've gotta be able to prove that he's lying.'

They strode across the foyer back to the desk and the still shaking clerk sat behind it. Fallen slammed both his hands on the desk and stared hard at the small man guarding the hotel register. The clerk got to his feet and forced a smile.

'I heard the ruckus, Marshal,' he said.

The marshal ignored the statement and leaned over towards the nervous hotel employee.

'Has that varmint in Room Three left the hotel during the last hour or so?' he asked.

The small clerk shook his head.

'Nope,' he replied.

'Are you sure, sonny?' Heck squinted at the clerk.

'If he wanted to leave the Diamond Pin he'd have to pass through the foyer, Marshal,' the clerk explained. 'You've got to pass this way even if you use the rear door. There ain't no other way out of here.'

'Damn it,' Fallen looked at his equally surprised deputy and then touched the brim of his hat to the clerk. 'Thank you kindly, son.'

They turned, and Fallen angrily led Heck towards the double doors. As he reached down and turned the brass handle he paused and looked back at the desk clerk.

'You'd best get someone to head on up there to replace the door to Room Three,' he said.

'What happened to the door, Marshal?' the small man asked.

'It kinda tangled with my boot,' Fallen answered, as he and his deputy left the hotel.

CHAPTER SIXTEEN

The man in black was no longer slurring his words. He stood and marched across the hotel room and pulled out his silver cigar case and opened its lid. He withdrew a fine Havana and carefully bit off its tail as he stared down at the lantern-lit street. After returning the case to his pocket he lit the cigar from the top of the table lamp's glass funnel. He pulled the lace drape from the window and started to chuckle as he watched both the lawmen heading back towards the funeral parlour.

They were perfect targets, but Ward had other plans. He reached up behind the curtain and pulled his blood-stained stiletto out of the wooden window frame. He was still chuckling as he slid the long knife down into the neck of his right boot.

'This is just too damn easy,' he laughed as smoke filtered between his teeth. 'How these mindless critters managed to capture brother Lucas and hang him, I'll never know.'

Ward pulled the cigar from his lips and exhaled a line of grey smoke at the lace drape before resting his hip on the edge of the table.

'Why would I kill the undertaker?' he repeated the words which he had so skilfully spoken to Marshal Fallen and his underling. He rammed the cigar back into his mouth and filled his lungs with strong smoke.

Ward then pulled out his billfold and extracted the fifty-dollar bank note that he had taken from Sam Foster after he had ripped his innards apart with his stiletto.

The banknote had traces of blood on it and the puncture holes where it had been pinned to the letter he had sent to the undertaker.

'Reckon Sam Foster won't be needing this where he's headed unless they've started charging entrance fees,' he chuckled as he returned the bill to the billfold. He folded its leather and slid it into the inside pocket of his trail coat.

He then reached down into his deep outer pocket and pulled out the handful of letters his brother had sent to him during his trial. Ward had memorized every word in them, but it was the top letter that he prioritized above all the others. He pulled it out of its envelope and unfolded the sheet of paper. His icy stare focused on the handwriting that Lucas had scrawled shortly before he was executed.

It was the final ranting of a mentally ill man who had totally lost his sanity and was blaming everyone else for his ultimate downfall. The letter had ignited within Jonas a trait that both of the Ward brothers shared: it had ignited the same demented murderous fuse in Jonas that Lucas had succumbed to years before.

Ward looked at the well-worn paper in his hand with avenging clarity. He stared through the cigar smoke at his brother's words in the same fashion that some folks would study their Bible. It was as though Lucas's lunacy was infectious, and was infecting the normally rational Jonas. In fact his brother's insanity had affected him far more than he realized, and the man who had never resorted to violence during his years of dare-devil robberies had now become as bad as his sibling.

Three names had been scrawled on the paper by Lucas, the names of three individuals who were totally unaware they had been branded as being responsible for not only getting Lucas caught, but also found guilty.

Jonas read out the final paragraph.

'Sam Foster the undertaker and foreman of the jury steered the jury into finding me guilty,' Ward read before casting his eyes on the two other names below it. 'Miss Betty LaRue, the owner of the Crimson Heart brothel, who could have given me an alibi, and Marshal Matt Fallen who captured me. They all should die for what they did to me. Avenge me, Brother Jonas.'

With the cigar firmly gripped in the corner of his

mouth, Ward found a two-inch pencil and stared at the three names that he had already started to eliminate. He licked the end of the pencil and drew a line through Sam's name, and then considered the other two names. Although Ward knew that Lucas had deserved to die for the atrocities he had perpetrated in countless towns before reaching War Smoke, the irrational bond that only kinship could muster had grown like a cancer inside his own mind.

Ward ran his thumbnail below the female's name.

'Next it's time for Miss LaRue to be punished for not giving Lucas an alibi,' Ward said as clouds of smoke surrounded his head. 'You don't know it yet, dear lady, but the sand is draining out of your hourglass faster than spit.'

Ward put the pencil back into his pocket and inhaled deeply on his Havana. He then carefully folded the letter and slid it back into its envelope and returned it with the others to his deep trail-coat pocket. He then picked up his long gunbelt and shook it loose, looped it around his hips and buckled it as he continued to watch Fallen and Heck enter the funeral parlour down the street. He reached down and tied the holster's leather lace around his thigh and then gazed back at the amber-lit street.

'It can't be too difficult to find a whore house in this stinking town,' Ward muttered as he cast a glance at the gaping hole where the room door had once stood. 'All you have to do is follow the stink of sweat and cheap perfume.'

He walked across the room to the bed and picked up his hat, and dusted it off before returning to the window. Although Ward did not realize it, he was turning into his late brother with every passing heart-beat.

'Time to find Miss Betty,' he muttered, putting on his Stetson and tightening its drawstring. He lifted the sash window and poked his long slim leg out on to the balcony. He stepped out into the crisp night air. 'And once I've found her I'll make that bitch pay.'

Ward still had the taste of death in his mouth, and he wanted to savour its acrid flavour again. He walked to the railings and rested his hands on its wooden top post and stared at the activity inside the funeral parlour.

He chuckled. War Smoke's lawmen would be busy for quite a while, he reasoned. Then he spotted the elderly figure of Doc Weaver making his way along Front Street to the funeral parlour with his trusty medical bag in his hand.

'You might as well slow up, old timer,' Ward whis-pered to the doctor from his high vantage point. 'Sam Foster is beyond your pathetic ability to help him.'

The man in black sniffed the air like a hound dog searching for an elusive fox. Many conflicting aromas travelled on the cool night air. One of them was the scent of stale perfume and powder. A depraved smile etched his face.

'I reckon all I've gotta do is follow my nose,' Ward said confidently as he stepped over the railing and faced the building next to the Diamond Pin. 'Follow the scent and you'll soon find the ladies it belongs to.'

Black, brooding clouds drifted over War Smoke, and for a few moments they blotted out the large moon. The settlement was suddenly blanketed in darkness. As the fleeting light of the moon momentarily reappeared, Ward was gone.

CHAPTER
SEVENTEEN

Jonas Ward knew that the greatest abundance of females selling their bodies was down near the cattle pens gathered along the rail tracks. He had spotted more glowing red lamps at that end of War Smoke than anywhere else when he had ridden through the labyrinth of streets and alleyways after leaving the resting locomotive.

Unseen and unheard, Ward raced across the roofs towards the place where he felt sure he might locate the grandest of all the whore houses. Nobody witnessed the agile man draped in black as he leapt and climbed over the rooftops at a speed that defied the laws of gravity as well as those of sanity.

Nothing could stop his vendetta.

Jonas Ward was hell bent on avenging the conviction and execution of his brother Lucas. He had already claimed the life of the first man his brother

Lucas had blamed for his demise, and now he was after the second name on the list: the feisty Miss Betty LaRue, whose only crime was to have told the truth, and to state under oath that Lucas Ward had not been with her at the time of his crimes.

Jonas Ward had vowed to kill them all as well as anyone else who might get in his way. He moved at almost inhuman speed across the array of wooden and brick structures towards the poorer part of War Smoke. The aroma of stale perfume and scented powder filled his flared nostrils as he reached the rooftops overlooking the shadowy streets and alleyways that spread out from the cattle pens near the stockyard like spiders' webs.

This part of town was markedly darker than the heart of War Smoke. Its only illumination came from the lanterns covered in red cloth. Ward negotiated the wooden shingles and leapt from one roof to another, and then descended to the ground. He landed in the shadows and looked around the eerily empty alley. He rose to his full height and pressed his back against a wall as his ice-cold eyes surveyed his unfamiliar surroundings.

The overpowering smell of cheap perfume dominated the darkness. Ward knew that he must be close to the place called the Crimson Heart, and once he found the infamous brothel it would be only a matter of time before he located Betty LaRue. The man in black moved away from the wall, crossed the dark alley and turned into a side street. The scent grew stronger with every step he took as he continued his search. Ward did not realize it, but he was searching for what was reputed to be the biggest and most lucrative of all the whore houses in War Smoke.

Ward emerged from the shadows and was still vainly continuing his search when a girl appeared out of one of the doorways ahead of him. She tilted her head as he approached, and expertly displayed her wares. The red lamp above the doorway flattered her, its almost pink light softening her appearance. She smiled coyly, and Ward touched his hat brim respectfully, but kept moving towards her. His long black trail-coat tails billowed in the gentle night breeze as he slowed his pace.

'Hello, stranger,' the heavily scented female cooed in a well rehearsed fashion. 'I ain't seen you along here before. Are you looking for a little fun?'

He stopped and eyed her from head to toe. She had seen better days, but he made no judgement of either her or the choice of occupation she plied.

'It's kinda late for a young girl to be out all alone,' he flattered her. 'You ought to go home before your momma misses you.'

She laughed and circled the lean man. 'You didn't answer me, handsome. I asked you if you wanted to have some fun. Do you?'

He pulled down the brim of his hat until it shielded his eyes from her and moved even closer. The closer he got, the less attractive she became.

'I'm kinda busy right now,' Ward said drily as he

looked at the ground. 'I was wondering, do you happen to know where the Crimson Heart is? I've got business there.'

The mere mention of the name of the town's biggest brothel seemed to sicken her. She moved even closer and pushed her exposed cleavage under his lowered head.

'Don't you want me to keep you company for a while?' she asked without answering his question. 'I can show you a real good time for half the price any of Miss Betty's girls will charge you.'

The name of the woman he sought caused Ward to raise his head and look straight into the girl's face.

'I'm not going to the Crimson Heart for that kinda business, ma'am,' Ward smiled, and allowed the girl to keep pushing herself into him as he dipped his hand into his trail coat pocket and fished out two silver dollars. The coins glinted beneath the red lamp as he teased the girl with them. 'I'm a drummer. I work for a big eastern company and they want me to finalize a deal for them.'

The girl kept trying to snatch the coins from his hands, but Ward was too fast for her. She smiled and pressed her heavily powdered and painted face into his as her fingers skilfully toyed with the drawstring of his black Stetson.

'Come on inside,' she cooed. 'You can go to Betty LaRue's place later. Come on.'

Ward sighed.

'I have to get some important papers signed

before morning, Missy,' he said, so convincingly that he almost believed it himself. 'Tell me where it is and I'll give you this money.'

She looked shocked. 'You'd give me them two bucks for just telling you where the Crimson Heart is?'

Ward nodded. 'I promise.'

She pointed along the dark street.

'Walk down to the corner and turn right,' she willingly informed. 'You can't miss the place. Very cheap looking, if you ask me.'

A smile filled his features. He placed the two silver dollars in the cleavage of her ample bosom and watched the coins disappear into her boned corset. She giggled as the cold metal coins continued their journey into the unknown folds of her undergarments.

'Thank you, ma'am,' Ward said as he moved away from her and headed to where she had told him he would find the brothel.

'Come on back when you're finished,' the girl waved at Ward's back. 'You can do business with me anytime you like.' As Ward reached the corner he glanced back at the girl standing beneath the red light.

'You wouldn't like my kinda business, Missy,' he whispered under his breath before continuing. 'It's kinda fatal.'

The man in black turned and had taken only three steps when he saw the brightly illuminated structure before him. He paused momentarily and produced a cigar from his silver case, and bit off its tip before spitting at the ground. A hundred options raced through his mind as he carefully placed the stout Havana in the corner of his mouth. He knew he could just walk into the structure and start shooting if he liked, but that was not the plan he had been mulling over for months. Miss Betty LaRue had to die, but first she had to know why she was being executed. Ward knew that he could not do that in War Smoke: that could only be achieved at Boot Hill.

A wry smile covered his face as he studied the structure. The Crimson Heart was totally unlike all the other places in War Smoke providing a similar service. Whereas they were small and barely noticeable apart from their traditional red lamps, the Crimson Heart was large and lit up like the 4 July. A couple of buckboards out front were filling the spaces not occupied by saddle horses. The sound of piano music wafted out from one of the open windows, and an untold number of contented voices also spilled out on to the street.

Ward ignited a match with his thumbnail, cupped its flame and filled his lungs with the acrid smoke he craved. He tossed the spent match at the sand and started across the narrow street towards the undoubtedly popular building. The closer he got to the Crimson Heart, the more determined Ward became to fulfil the wishes his brother had written in his last letter.

He stopped outside the busy structure and studied

132

the two-storey building. It seemed that each of the rooms behind the windows was occupied and by the sound of it, folks were having themselves a good time.

Ward's eyes darted across the structure. Then they focused on the open doorway and the well-lit interior. He tapped ash from his Havana and then pushed it back into the corner of his mouth and proceeded up the three stone steps to the entrance.

He had only just set foot inside the building when a woman's voice drew his attention. He glanced from under the flat brim of his hat at the mature woman who was walking towards him.

'And what do you want, handsome?' she asked.

Jonas Ward smiled and studied the buxom lady, probably in her forties and obviously in charge of the Crimson Heart.

'I'm looking for a certain lady named Miss Betty LaRue,' he replied in his most seductive of voices. 'You wouldn't happen to be Betty, would you?'

She fluttered her long eyelashes at the lean man.

'I sure would, handsome,' the notorious Miss Betty LaRue was clad in a revealing yet expensive dress. Her large breasts were contained in its dark blue silk and supported in a way that enabled them to bounce with every word she uttered. She was attractive, and Ward could tell that she must have been beautiful at one time. 'What do you want of me?'

He removed his hat and gave a polite bow before returning his Stetson to his head. 'It's an honour to meet you, Miss Betty.'

She was suspicious of the handsome stranger, mainly because she could sense that he was dangerous. Yet even so, she was attracted to him. Danger had always intrigued her.

'Don't go wasting your time sweet talking me, friend,' Betty LaRue said as he stepped closer to her. 'You ain't getting no discount with any of my gals.'

Ward shook his head.

'You misunderstand me, dear lady,' he smiled. 'I'm not interested in mere girls. If I have a choice I always throw my hat at the more mature ladies.'

She leaned back and studied the stranger.

'You look familiar,' she said. 'Have we ever tangled before?'

'I'm afraid not,' Ward grinned. 'I was sent to War Smoke by my bosses back east to find you and propose a deal which I'm led to believe would make you one of the wealthiest ladies in the state.'

'I've already got more money than I know what to do with, pretty boy,' she smiled as her eyes continued to study the stranger more carefully.

'This is a special deal designed just for you, Miss Betty,' Ward said before exhaling smoke at the ceiling.

'A deal?' she repeated. 'Are you a drummer?'

'Hardly, I pretend to be a simple drummer, but in fact I represent one of the largest companies in New York.' Ward continued to spin his tall tale. 'I understand that one of my bosses might have bumped into you several years ago. Because of this he wanted you to be the first to profit by the company's next venture.'

'What's your name, handsome?' Betty asked.

Ward had to do some quick thinking. He drew on his cigar and then blew the smoke at the floorboards as his mind raced.

'They call me Jonas,' he said.

She moved closer to him and fingered his bandanna. 'Is that your first or last name?'

'Both,' he smiled.

Betty LaRue laughed. 'You're being mighty careful with your words, Jonas. What's the name of your boss?'

'I'm afraid I can't tell you that yet,' Ward looked around them. Not one person was paying either of them the slightest notice.

'What's this deal you was talking about?' she asked.

Ward pulled the cigar from his lips and tapped its ash on to the floor and then looked at her. 'I can't tell you here, but if you would come with me I'll show you.'

The normally cautious woman took the bait. She moved around him and ran a long fingernail across his shoulders, then reached over her desk and plucked a crimson shawl off the pink cushion that adorned her chair close to the entrance.

She winked at the stranger.

'Come on, Jonas,' she purred like a kitten. 'My buggy is just around the corner. You can drive me to wherever it is you want to take me.'

He followed her out into the street. Her swaying hips moved seductively and the man in black willingly followed. They stopped when they reached the boardwalk at the bottom of the steps. Miss Betty LaRue glanced at Ward.

'My buggy is just around the corner,' she repeated, before adding, 'It's the one with a black gelding between its traces.'

Ward nodded and walked to get the vehicle.

One of her muscular staff moved from the shadows and leaned down so that his words could not be overheard.

'You sure you wanna take a ride with that fella, Miss Betty?' he asked the owner of the Crimson Heart. 'He looks like trouble to me.'

Betty LaRue smiled. 'I can handle him, Dan.'

CHAPTER EIGHTEEN

Doc Weaver had just completed his examination of the dead body in the funeral parlour and had made his way out into the street to wash his hands in the water trough when his attention was drawn to the clattering approach of the most expensive buggy in War Smoke. He stood with his shirt sleeves rolled up to his elbows as the vehicle came into view. His wrinkled eyes squinted hard at the buggy and its occupants as the black gelding raced through the moonlight, then turned the corner and headed out of town.

'Was that who I think it was, Doc?' Elmer asked as he ambled out beside the elderly medical man holding Doc's battered tweed coat. Doc dipped his arms into the ice-cold water and washed the gore off his skin. He shook his hands and then started to roll his sleeves back down.

'I dunno, Elmer,' he grumbled. 'Who did you think it was?'

'It sure looked like Miss Betty from the Crimson Heart in that buggy,' Elmer scratched his head. 'Though I ain't ever seen that lean dude with her before.'

'Me neither, boy,' agreed Doc, and accepted the deputy's assistance to put his coat back on. 'He was sure whipping that black horse up a storm, though.'

'It seems a tad late for Miss Betty to go driving with a man young enough to be her son, don't it?' Elmer mused as he continued to watch the moonlit dust hanging in the night air.

Doc raised a bushy eyebrow. 'Just how do you know who Miss Betty is, Elmer boy?'

Even the amber lantern light could not conceal the blushing cheeks of the young deputy. Elmer gave a coy grin and shrugged as Matt Fallen walked out of the funeral parlour and stood between the pair.

'What you sparring about now, boys?' Fallen asked as he rested his knuckles on his hips.

'Elmer here was telling me how he knew Miss Betty, Matt,' Doc teased as Heck ambled out with the medical bag. 'He even knows the name of her place down yonder.'

Fallen looked intrigued.

'What about Miss Betty?' he asked, as Heck handed the small black bag to Doc. Fallen looked at Elmer. 'Why would you start talking about her for?'

'She was in a buggy being driven out of town, Marshal Fallen,' Elmer pointed to the direction the

138

horse-drawn vehicle had taken.

'That woman is gonna catch her death,' Heck interrupted. 'Her chest is always uncovered no matter what the weather.'

Fallen gently slapped the back of Elmer's head to get the deputy's attention.

'Who was driving her buggy?' he asked.

Elmer raised his shoulders. 'I never seen him before, Marshal Fallen. He was dressed all in black, and the way he was using that whip he was sure in a hurry.'

'Kinda dumb to drive any sort of vehicle at that speed at night, Matt,' Doc drily commented as he searched for his pipe. 'Whoever that fella was, he was sure in a damn hurry.'

Fallen stared long and hard at the youngster.

'Are you sure he was all in black, Elmer?' he pressed.

'The boy's right, Matt,' Doc nodded as he rubbed his moustache. 'The driver of that buggy was all in black. Like a damn undertaker.'

Heck moved closer to the marshal.

'Do you figure it's that wine-drinking varmint we talked to a while back, Matthew?' he asked.

Matt Fallen gave a firm nod of his head. 'There's only one way to find out. C'mon, Heck.'

Doc put his pipe stem in his mouth and looked to Elmer as both Fallen and Heck ran from the funeral parlour to the grand hotel halfway along Front Street.

'Now what do you reckon has them two boys so all fired up, Elmer?' he asked the deputy.

Elmer scratched his head. 'Wish I knew, Doc.'

CHAPTER NINETEEN

The pair of lawmen did not slow their pace until they reached the boardwalk outside the Diamond Pin Hotel. Matt Fallen exhaled loudly as he stepped up on to the wooden boards, and paused for a brief moment. A few heartbeats later Heck caught up with the long-legged marshal, just stopping to adjust his pants and his wayward holster.

'Just a cotton-picking minute there, Matthew,' Heck moaned as he tightened the rope holding up his pants and dragged the holster on to his hip. 'My britches almost fell down.'

As Fallen took a stride towards the hotel's double doors, one of them opened and the small clerk stepped out into the night air. He halted and stared at the two men with tin stars walking towards him.

'I was just heading over to your office, Marshal,' he said. 'That man in Room Three ain't there any longer.'

Fallen pushed his hat back and moved closer to

the hotel clerk. The lanterns to either side of the hotel entrance lit his face in its amber light.

'Ward ain't in his room?' he questioned.

'Nope, he's gone,' the small man replied. 'I sent a couple of men to replace the door, and when they came back down they told me the room was empty.'

Heck ambled in between the two men.

'Did you see that galoot pass your desk, sonny?' he asked.

The small figure shook his head. 'Nobody passed my desk. I've bin there since you left the hotel.'

Fallen stroked his rugged jaw.

'Were your men sure that Ward wasn't in his room?'

'They were certain,' the clerk retorted. 'They did say that the window was open, though.'

'That *hombre* must be using the window to come and go, Matthew,' Heck suggested. 'He must be part monkey.'

'But there's no staircase to the balcony,' the clerk noted.

Fallen and Heck looked at one another and then stepped down on to the sand and looked up to the balcony. The deputy rubbed his neck and shook his head in disbelief as Fallen studied the high balcony carefully.

'He must have left and returned to his room that way,' he drawled. 'That's a mighty high balcony though.'

Heck walked to the side of the marshal and bit his

lip as they both looked upwards. 'Are you reckoning that Ward somehow jumped from up there and then climbed back up, Matthew?'

Fallen nodded. 'It's the only way he could have done it, Heck. That's why the clerk never saw him leave.'

Heck raised both his eyebrows.

'So he could have bin the critter that killed old Sam,' he reasoned, with a long sigh. 'He hood-winked us.'

Matt Fallen looked to the clerk and touched his hat brim to him. 'Thanks, friend. You've just solved a puzzle that's bin gnawing at my guts.'

'I'm glad I could help, Marshal,' the clerk went back into the hotel.

Heck looked at his towering friend.

'So that must have been Ward that Doc and Elmer saw driving Miss Betty out of town, Matthew,' the deputy noted, scratching his beard thoughtfully. 'I wonder where he was taking her in such a hurry?'

Suddenly Matt Fallen's expression altered from one of confusion to one of trepidation. He looked at the thoughtful deputy and slapped his hands together.

'That loco-bean is taking her to Boot Hill, Heck,' he said.

'Why in tarnation would he be taking her all the way up there at this time of night, Matthew?' Heck wondered.

There was only one possible explanation as far as

143

the rugged marshal could see. His eyes darted at his deputy.

'To kill her and fill one of those graves, Heck,' Fallen replied, and then swung on his heels. 'Get the horses. We've gotta get to Boot Hill before he kills again.'

CHAPTER TWENTY

Miss Betty LaRue had relished the thrill of the fast and feverish ride up to Boot Hill; her heart had not beaten so quickly for decades. She had not sensed the danger in the man seated next to her in the buggy. Nor had she feared that same stranger in black as he had practically dragged her from the expensive vehicle once they had entered the cemetery.

Miss Betty had weathered many storms during her life, as had all ladies who had chosen the same profession. Nothing frightened her, and had not done so for the longest time.

Even as Ward had held her small hand tightly and led her across the graveyard she had laughed at the impending thrill she anticipated. There was something inside her which was actually flattered and excited by the younger man. For years she had not been the focus of any of her clients' attention, and Ward's urgency had rekindled a fire which she had thought was long dormant.

For the first time in many, many years, Miss Betty was the centre of a man's desire.

At least that was what she had thought.

The fleeting memory of what it felt like to be young again had blinkered Miss Betty against the reality of the situation she now found herself in.

But her excitement was to be short lived.

After Miss Betty LaRue had looked around the deserted graveyard she suddenly became aware that Ward was no longer smiling. She fanned her red cheeks with her tiny hands and looked at his emotionless glare.

'You're not smiling any more, handsome,' Betty said as she suddenly noticed the three freshly dug graves at her feet. Her eyes stared into his face. For a terrifying moment she wondered why he had brought her to Boot Hill. Her throat suddenly became dry as she stared at the man in black.

'Why have you brought me here, Jonas?' she asked, as he looked at her from under the brim of his hat. 'What was the business deal you talked about back at the Crimson Heart?'

Ward smiled. It was not the smile of someone who was about to share anything humourous. He tilted his head and stared at her, and then stepped closer.

'My name is Jonas Ward, Miss Betty,' he revealed. 'And there ain't no business deal.'

For a moment the name meant nothing to her – and then she recalled another man who shared the same surname – a murderer who had preyed upon innocent girls who were unable to defend themselves.

Miss Betty's heart pounded beneath her finery.

'Ward?' she gasped as the memory of Lucas Ward flashed through her mind. She then recognized the resemblance between the man in black and Lucas Ward. She shied away from Ward like someone who has just caught sight of a monster. Loose soil under her shoes slipped away, and she almost fell into one of the deep graves. Somehow she managed to steady herself, and her expression changed as she glanced from Ward to the graves.

'Take me back,' the buxom woman demanded.

'You're starting to remember my dear brother,' Ward said, as he pushed his long trail coat over the holstered grip of his .45. 'I can see it in your face. No amount of paint can hide the guilt you feel for not helping Lucas.'

Miss Betty's eyes flashed at the man that had tricked her.

'Lucas wanted me to say that he was in the Crimson Heart at the time of each of the murders!' she exclaimed as the severity of coming to this remote place dawned on her.

'Why wouldn't you give Brother Lucas an alibi?' Ward snarled. 'Why not?'

Miss Betty inhaled deeply and squared up to Ward.

'Why not?' she repeated before angrily shaking a fist at him. 'Listen, I don't lie for anyone, especially mindless killers. Your brother got what he deserved when they lynched him!'

Without warning, Ward sprang towards her like a mountain cat. His hands struck her ample bosom and knocked her off balance: Betty LaRue toppled back and suddenly fell into one of the deep holes.

Ward drew his six-shooter from its holster and glanced over the edge of the six-foot-deep chasm. For a moment the blackest of shadows hid her from view. Then he could see her struggling to get back to her feet. The fall had winded her and covered her in mud. Her elaborate dress with its multitude of underskirts hampered her from achieving anything apart from repeatedly stepping on its hem and tripping over.

'Get me out of here,' she screamed.

Ward shook his head and aimed his gun at her. 'That would be pointless, you whore. You're exactly where I intended for you to be. In your grave.'

'My grave?'

Even the layers of make-up on her face could not hide the terror she felt at hearing his words. Betty looked up from the deep hole she was trapped in and shook her head in disbelief.

'You can't just kill me,' she exclaimed.

'I can and I will,' Ward disagreed.

'But why would you wanna kill me?' Betty had backed away as far as the damp dirt wall. Yet she was still staring up into the barrel of his ominous six-gun. 'All I did was tell the truth.'

Ward narrowed his eyes.

'Brother Lucas had his demons, Miss Betty,' he admitted. 'But he was my brother and I loved him. You failed him in his hour of need, and for that you must pay.'

Miss Betty shielded her eyes and awaited the inevitable as she sensed that her time was about to end. She was about to scream, when Boot Hill resounded to the ear-splitting noise of a gun shot.

FINALE

Totally stunned by the shot that had whistled past his head, Jonas Ward looked up and saw the two approaching riders as they carved a frantic trail through the moonlight towards Boot Hill. The demented man in black could see the tin stars pinned to their chests and the gunsmoke trailing from Matt Fallen's drawn six-shooter.

Fallen fired again. The marshal's bullet ricocheted off the most impressive tombstone in the cemetery and sent shards of debris up into the night air.

'It's those damned star-packers,' Ward growled, and then blasted back at the lawmen. He ran down to where there were a few large stone markers and dropped down behind one of them. He pressed his shoulder into the moss-covered stone and fired frantically at the advancing lawmen.

Undeterred, Fallen ducked under the neck of his galloping mount and then fired again. He straightened back up on his saddle and spurred the grey gelding on towards Boot Hill as Heck guided his mule to the opposite side of the cemetery.

The marshal leapt from his mount and then ran for cover as bullets cut through the eerie moonlight after him. Heck rode straight towards the picket fencing encircling the graveyard. As Fallen fanned his gun hammer he watched in total amazement as his deputy managed to get his mule to leap over the moonlit fence.

Inside the cemetery the mule stumbled, and Fallen winced as Heck tumbled off the back of his saddle and rolled across the muddy ground until he hit a sturdy wooden marker. Stunned, Heck watched as his angry mule bucked and kicked its way through the graveyard.

'Are you OK, Heck?' the marshal shouted as bullets cut through the air to either side of his crouching frame.

'I reckon so, Matthew,' the dazed deputy answered.

Ward turned his attention on the deputy and fired furiously at Heck. Large chunks of wood were torn off the grave marker as the man in black emptied his six-shooter at his stunned target. Sawdust fell like snow over Heck's crawling body as Ward swiftly shook the spent casings from his gun and started refilling its hot chambers with bullets from his gunbelt.

'You made a real bad mistake coming up here, Fallen,' Ward yelled out as he turned on his knees to where he had last seen the marshal. 'You're next on my list.'

The lawman reloaded his .45 and considered the words of the man they had come to prevent adding to his tally. He closed the smoking chamber of his six-shooter and looked long and hard for his elusive prey.

'What you talking about, Ward?' Matt Fallen yelled out at the top of his voice as he cocked his gun's hammer. 'What list would that be?'

'My brother's killing list, Marshal,' Ward replied before leaning around the grave stone and firing at Fallen. 'He wrote to me telling me the names of the three folks that got him hanged.'

As Ward rested his back against the largest grave-stone in the cemetery he saw the deputy's mule kicking and bucking around Boot Hill like a snorting bull. Ward raised his gun and aimed his nickel-plated six-shooter at the bucking mule.

'Whatever that animal is, I'm gonna kill it before it gets too close,' he said, and fired. But the shot nicked one of the mule's ears and sent it into an even greater rage. Even though laden with a hefty saddle and all its master's trappings, the bucking animal still managed to leap off the ground and kick out with all its hoofs at the same time.

Fallen slid down through some tall grass and started to make his way round the graveyard so as to get behind Jonas Ward. Ward rose up another few inches and held his gun at arm's length as he aimed

152

at the crazed mule. The moonlight reflected off the gun's nickel plating: it was like a beacon, and the mule charged straight towards it.

Ward fired steadily at the mule and at Fallen.

Wooden markers and solid stones were trampled beneath the crazed animal's hoofs as it careered through the cemetery towards the lit-up gun and the man who had shot a chunk off its ear.

Heck got up on to his knees and stared in horror at his mule racing through the moonlight towards the ruthless killer.

'Quit that, Nellie,' Heck shouted at his demented mule. But the mule kept charging on. 'Damn it all, Nellie.'

Fallen reached the far side of Boot Hill, and was wading up through the swaying high grass to where he knew Ward was secreted, when a volley of shots cut through the eerie light. Fallen felt one of the shots graze his shoulder: it was like being jabbed by a branding iron. The marshal dropped down on to his belly as another bullet ripped through his Stetson and tore it from his head.

'You're trapped, Fallen,' Ward laughed out loud.

The marshal knew that he was pinned down. He could not go forward, and doubted that his large frame would get far if he tried to retreat: he was a big target, and he knew it.

'Don't fret none, Matthew,' Heck shouted out from across the cemetery. 'I'll get that rascal.'

The deputy started to blast his hefty Army Colt in

Ward's direction. Two shots hit the tombstone in front of Ward and sent chunks of grit cascading over him. As Ward ducked, Fallen levelled his smoking six-shooter at him: he squeezed his trigger and sent a fiery rod of lethal venom straight across the distance between them.

The bullet caught Ward in his chest.

The chilling sound that came from Ward's mouth was like something formed in the bowels of Hell itself. The man in black rose to his feet and blasted his gun as pain tore through his body.

Fallen raced across the graveyard until he found another group of markers to hunch behind. He pulled on his trigger again and sent his last bullet at Ward. The man in black buckled as it hit him dead centre.

Like a wounded animal, Ward swung his gun and unleashed the last of its bullets before collapsing on his knees. The empty six-gun fell from his grasp as his watery eyes looked in all directions.

Suddenly out of nowhere, the mule came crashing back through the pair of lawmen. Both Fallen and Heck were sent cart-wheeling as the furious animal bucked passed them and continued round the cemetery on towards the man who had taken a chunk out of one of its ears.

Fallen winced at the sound of the scream.

It was hideous and gut-wrenching. Fallen lunged at the mule but was forced to retreat when the injured animal kicked out its back legs feverishly.

'Quit that, Nellie gal,' Heck vainly shouted before turning to the marshal and shrugging. 'There ain't no talking to that mule when she's hurt, Matthew. She gets plumb ornery.'

Fallen patted his friend on the shoulder.

'She's got the right to be ornery, Heck,' he said. 'Ward shot a lump out of her ear. I reckon I might get a tad tetchy as well if he'd done that to me.'

Both lawmen watched helplessly as the mule kept pounding its hoofs into the ground. Blood was spread out in sickening splatters from Ward's remains. The pitiful whimpering had stopped long before the mule ceased its deadly actions. Matt Fallen and his sidekick stared down at what was left of Jonas Ward. He was unrecognisable.

'At least Nellie saved the town the cost of another trial, Heck,' Fallen said bluntly as he checked his wound. 'I'll buy her an apple tomorrow.'

'Is you hurt bad, Matthew?' Heck asked as he edged towards his tiring mule.

'Nope, just a graze, Heck,' Fallen replied as they cautiously edged towards the fallen Jonas Ward. Heck grabbed the reins of his mule as the tall marshal stared down at the body of the dangerous assassin.

Heck looked around at the damage caused to the cemetery on Boot Hill by the mule running amok. 'Most of the markers ain't where they're meant to be, Matthew. The town council will sure be mighty angry about this.'

'We'll say that Ward did it, Heck,' Fallen winked.

Heck grinned and patted the nose of the still snorting animal. 'Ain't that nice of Matthew, Nellie? He's gonna tell a big fib for you.'

The lofty marshal stared down at the body of the man in black and spat. He stretched up to his full height and gazed around the cemetery.

'I wonder where Ward left poor old Miss Betty's body,' he mumbled thoughtfully.

'We'd best check them empty graves, Matthew,' Heck secured the mule's reins to the picket fence and walked up to Fallen. 'I got me a sneaky feeling that one of them holes ain't empty no longer.'

'Yeah, you're right, Heck.' Fallen nodded.

Both men started walking to where they knew the three fresh graves had been dug. Neither was in a hurry to see what Ward might have done to Betty LaRue.

'That varmint sure was determined to kill somebody,' muttered Heck as they neared the three mounds of earth that were piled up close to the graves. Then the unnerving sound of a female voice coming from the freshly dug graves surprised both him and his deputy. Heck grabbed Fallen's arm.

'Did you hear that cussing, Matthew?' Heck asked his tall companion. 'Sounds like we done woke up a ghost.'

'That ain't no ghost, Heck,' Fallen hurriedly strode through the debris to where the shouting was coming from. Heck was close behind his superior.

156

They looked down into the closest hole. All he could see was the muddy face of Miss Betty LaRue. 'Howdy, Miss Betty.'

Fallen rubbed his jaw as he studied the buxom woman. He had never seen her look anything but pristine. As mud dripped from her he had to grit his teeth not to burst out laughing.

'Nice evening for a buggy ride, Miss Betty,' he commented. She frowned at the tall lawman.

'Did you kill him, Marshal?' she asked holding her hands up to the grinning Fallen. 'Pull me out of here before some short-sighted bastard fills this hole in.'

Heck stood on his toes and whispered to Fallen. 'She sure looks a mess, Matthew. Why that Ward *hombre* would want to come up here with a woman in that condition beats the tar out of me.'

'I heard that, Longfellow,' Miss Betty LaRue growled.

Fallen leaned over and stretched out his arms. 'Hold on to my hands and I'll lift you out of there, ma'am.'

'You didn't answer me, Marshal,' she said in a hushed tone. 'Is that young maniac dead?'

'He's dead all right, Miss Betty,' Matt Fallen leaned down, grabbed her wrists and pulled her back to the surface. She stood as mud dripped from her hair and dress. Miss Betty LaRue was a sorry sight by any standards.

'It's kinda messy down there, Marshal,' Betty said as she hitched up her ripped and torn dress and began to follow the lawman back to where the deputy had retreated. She stopped beside Heck and stared down at the body of Jonas Ward. 'That critter sweet talked me and I actually fell for it. There's no fool like an old fool.'

'You ain't that old, Miss Betty,' Heck tried to reassure her. 'Hell, you ain't anywhere near as old as my mother was when she up and died.'

Fallen looked at the expression on the woman's enraged face and could sense that she was close to start fighting. He sighed and touched his hat brim. 'I'd best go round up my horse and your buggy and then we'll escort you back to town, Miss Betty.'

'Thank you, Marshal,' she said.

Heck moved towards her.

'We've gotta escort you, Miss Betty,' he said. 'You ain't in no state to drive yourself. Look at you. You're a darn mess.'

Miss Betty LaRue had been simmering but was now beginning to boil over. 'I'm a mess?'

'You sure are. Don't fret none though, I'll drive you, Miss Betty,' Heck faced the notorious owner of the Crimson Heart and removed his hat. He then started to wipe the mud off her ample bosom with the tail of his scarf. 'Let me clean you up a tad.'

Miss Betty watched as Heck continued to stroke her wobbling breasts with his scarf. Her eyes narrowed and her eyebrows rose as she observed him happily removing the mud from her soft flesh. She cleared her throat in a vain bid to get Heck's attention. He then used his thumb and index finger to pick off bits of grass and twigs from her ample bosom.

'You got bits of all sorts stuck on you,' he noted before closing one eye and squinting down her cleavage. 'It wouldn't surprise me if'n I don't come across a branch or two down there, ma'am.'

The deputy blissfully continued.

'You don't have to thank me, Miss Betty,' Heck grinned happily, entranced by her feminine assets. 'It's a pleasure just being able to help a handsome lady like you get all cleaned up. This ain't a chore and I'm happy to do it. I'm a special deputy and we can do all sorts of things.'

Miss Betty traced a long fingernail down the side of his cheek and smiled, then leaned close to his left ear.

'You and the marshal might have saved my life, Heck,' she purred quietly, 'but if you keep doing that I'm gonna geld you just like they done to the marshal's horse. Savvy?'

'I was just trying to help,' he gulped.

'Help yourself, you mean, Longfellow,' she snorted.

Heck stopped, stepped back and swallowed hard.

'Yes, ma'am,' he gulped. 'I'd best go get your buggy.'

Matt Fallen led his grey horse and the buggy into the cemetery, and looked at both of their faces in turn.

'How's everything going?' he grinned.

'Everything's just dandy, Marshal,' Miss Betty smiled as she started towards her buggy. 'You can drive me home.'

Heck waited for her to be out of earshot, and then whispered out of the corner of his mouth:

'Whatever you do, don't try to stroke the mud off her chest, Matthew,' he warned. 'It makes her plumb ornery.'